THE MISSING CHILD

WENDY ELMER

authorHOUSE®

AuthorHouse™
1663 Liberty Drive
Bloomington, IN 47403
www.authorhouse.com
Phone: 1-800-839-8640

First published by AuthorHouse 7/1/2011

ISBN: 978-1-4634-1628-7 (sc)
ISBN: 978-1-4634-1627-0 (e)

Library of Congress Control Number: 2011910314

Printed in the United States of America

1

THE DAY OF John Reyes' release from prison was an exciting one for all involved in his life. He woke up excited and had an early breakfast. Warden Mary Kelly directed the prison guards to escort him through the procedure. He packed up his bedding sheets and TV set. He was given his own clothes back that he arrived in. He had to be drug tested one last time. He was put in a single cell and told to sit down. He was given two hundred dollars to start his life over. Mary Kelly asked him if he had any last minute questions. He said no madam and thank you for putting up with him. Mary Kelly wished him well and god speed.

2

JOHN WAS DRIVEN the eight hour trip from the jail to Las Vegas, Nevada. He was dropped off at the beginning of the strip at a Motel 6. It was across the street from the Mandalay Bay. The guards wished him well and took off back to California. He entered the office and asked for a room.

He said: "Good evening sir. I am just moving to Las Vegas and need to rent a room until I get on my feet."

The manager said: "Maybe we can work something out. You can stay here for free if you can be a handyman. Report to the office at 8:00 tomorrow morning and you can start then. For now take room 1 and have a hot shower. You will feel much better once you have a hot meal and a good night's sleep."

John said: "Thank you sir. Where can I get something to eat for dinner tonight?"

The manager said: "Two doors down we have a Burger King. You can bring that order to your room and have a nice feast." That is exactly what he did. After dinner and a shower he felt like a new man. He felt totally rejuvenated.

3

THE NEXT MORNING at precisely 8:00 John entered the office for work. The manager said: "Good morning John. Please tell me about yourself."

John was at first reluctant to talk about himself. Finally he started to talk and told him about himself. He admitted just getting out of jail for car stealing. He explained that he was trying to start his life over and do it right this time.

The manager asked: "Why did you choose to relocate to Las Vegas?"

John said: "It was my old cell mate that committed a horrific crime. I don't know whatever happened to him. I went to testify at a trial and turned him in. I met some very nice police detectives who believed me and actually listed to me. There are really nice people here. I wanted to be a part of that world." A week after he started John asked if there was any chance of him getting his own apartment. The manager made a phone call to his landlord and sure enough there was a one bedroom apartment available. They drove up to the complex called The Chantel. The apartment was on the second floor. The rent was very affordable because the heat from the Las Vegas sun in mid afternoon beat down and almost cooked the ceiling. He took one look at it and took it on the spot. On the first Saturday John made a trip to the supermarket and did his first official food shopping for his new apartment. He met Detective Shapiro down the bread aisle. Amazingly he remembered John from a previous encounter the year before.

Detective Shapiro said: "John, tell me about yourself. I heard you got out."

John said: "Yes sir. I just got out last week. I got a job at the Motel 6 as a handyman. I am working the front desk and doing whatever needs to be done. After work I go for a walk on the strip and get to know where to find what. The hotel guests ask me where to find certain things. My boss found me this new apartment. This is my first official shopping trip. My second day here I opened up my own savings account and checking account. I am well on the road to self sufficiency."

Detective Shapiro said: "I am very glad to hear it. Are you making any plans for supporting yourself?"

John said: "I am so happy to have a job and new friends that I haven't really thought about it."

Detective Shapiro said: "May I suggest becoming a cop? The exam is coming up next month and we are always looking for new recruits."

John asked: "Do I really qualify for being a cop? After all I do have a criminal record."

Detective Shapiro said: "You are not a convicted felon, just a misdemeanor. That means you do qualify."

After talking it over with his boss John went out and brought a manual to study for the police exam. Amazingly he passed on the first try. He scored ninety-five out of one hundred. For the next five months John put his body through paces he never thought he was capable of. He did not life standing on a pedastel with a baton. The goal was to knock your opponent off. He kept losing his balance and falling off. That was the only part of the training he did not excel at. He loved the jogging in place and running around the complex. There was talk among the officials of making him a teacher of the next class. His all time favorite was the horse training. He got a taste of being a mounted cop. Graduation consisted of ringing a bell. He was first in line because his grades were the highest in the class. Detective Shapiro was there to high five him when he came back. Everybody was lined up against the wall waiting their turn. John's first assignment was to be on street patrol. That was a little scary for him. He never knew what he was running in to.

Six months into his career John was called into the sergeant's office for a special assignment. He was being sent to school for special training to become a mounted cop. Amazingly the horse bonded immediately with John. He put is head down and wanted to be scratched on the snout. The proper way of approaching a horse is from the side because he can't see in front of him. The blinders are on his eyes to keep the bugs out of his eyes. The proper way of mounting is to put the left foot into the stirrup and swing the right leg over. John got confused between the left and right foot. Fortunately the sergeant was very patient with him. It was his first screw up. The first time he mounted John ended up facing the tail end of the horse. Eveybody is entitled to a mistake every once in a while. John and the seargeant both cracked up with hilarity when John managed that one. It took thirty minutes to get serious. Even tehe horse was making laughing noises. The seargeant explained the noise was called whinnying. He is just having fun with everybody else. When the horse jumps up on two legs that is called bucking.

4

ALL DURING THE time of John's training he had to go home and sleep each night. He couldn't move from exhaustion. He took to eating microwave dinners. Each night it was dinner in ten minutes a quick shower and then bed. On the weekends he was off from training, but he put in a full day of handy man at the Motel 6. He couldn't wait for Saturdays first for rest and then to share his week with the manager. For the first time in John's life he thought he ad direction and a reason to get up in the morning. He wouldn't have traded it for anything. The manager convinced him to start going to Church on Saturday nights.

5

ON St. Patrick's day there was a parade through the strip. That was pure chaos already because the college kids were off on break. They came to Las Vegas to drink and get stupid.

Just off the strip was St. Mark's Roman Catholic Church. Alice and her daughter Jessica went to pray for Alice's father who had a massive stroke. Alice needed guidance as to whether or not to take her father off life support. While she was praying Jessica snuck off to the confessional and then to the sacristy. The bagpipes blaring outside brought Alice out of her reveries and looked for Jessica. She was nowhere to be found. Alice started to panic and ran off to the rectory to find a priest. Everybody thought they turned the church upside down to look for her. The prist even looked inside the boiler. Luckily it was empty. Alice was told to sit in the back pew and not to move. A uniformed officer was posted next to her to make sure she didn't get lost too. The priest called the cops. Luckily Detective Shapiro and his team were right down the street. They were on security detail for the parade. The three of them flew into the church within 90 seconds of the call. He was called in because everyone knew he was an altar boy at the church and is still an active parishoner. The team entered the church and blessed themselves with Holy Water. They took a minute to comb their hair and look descent for entering God's House. They were met at the back of the church by Father Raaser the current pastor. They genuflected at the altar rail and blessed themselves again. They were brought into the sacristy for a briefing about the situation. Apparently Alice was praying for her father and that is when Jessica wandered off to parts unknown. They heard a very peculiar sound coming from the church. Fther Raaser assured them that the church was an old building just groaning. They went out back into the church and almost fainted from shock and surprise. There was John on a horse kneeling at the altar rail.

Detective Shapiro screamed out: "WHO IN BLUE BLAZES CALLED OUT THE MOUNTED POLICE? WHICH PART OF THIS EVEN REMOTELY LOOKS LIKE WE NEED A HORSE??!!!"

John said: "Take a freaking chill pill Shapiro. It is not that bad. I was patrolling the parade when the call came in about a missing child."

Shapiro looked at Father Raaser and saw him making goo-goo noises and tickling the horse. He was having a grand old time playing with it. It was no wonder his Confirmation name was Francis, names after St. Francis of Assissi. He explained that he recognized the horse from previous parish functions. The spring carnival from the year before had horse back riding. John declared that as soon as the horse heard St. Mark's Church the horse took off like a rocket.

Shapiro said: "Raaser, pleas focus!!! First we have to search every inch on this church from the basement boards up to the rafters." Him and Detective John Scanlon did that along with Father Raaser as the escort. All three of them searched and triple searched. Shapiro was informed that Jessica was afraid of the dark, so chances were very slim that she would be found in the confessionals. They searched anyway. Ain the sacristy they emptied the closet of all the chausibles and stolls handing up. The emptied the closet of the ropes that went around the waist to make sure she didn't hang herself by accident. They searched the boiler room and the boiler. Nothing was in there. Their next step was to bring Alice down to the precinct for an interview. It couldn't be done in the church because it was declared a crime scene.

6

A LICE WAS DRIVEN down to the precinct by Detective John Scanlon. Alice was given a hot meal and a bottle of water. She ate, but barely tasted any of it. The interview was conducted with a tape recorder. This way there was no question about what was said.

John Scanlon asked: "What is your full name?"

Alice said: "My full name is Alice McMann."

John asked: "Do you know what happened to Jessica today?"

Alice said: "No sir I don't know what happened to her."

John said: "That is what we are here to figure out. Tell me everything that happened today with you and Jessica. Start with when she woke up."

Alice said: "Jessica is four years old and she isn't in pre-K yet. She was rejected at the interview. I woke up Jessica at 7:00 this morning. Our morning routine is potty and brushing the teeth. After that she came into the kitchen and sat down to a breakfast of corn flakes and apple juice. Motts apple jurce is the only one she will drink."

John said: "Let me interrupt you right here. What excuse did they give you to reject Jessica from pre-school?"

Alice said: She was rejected because she didn't speak enough or clearly enough. They said she wasn't ready for school."

John said: "Okay continue Alidde. What did you do after breakfast?"

Alice said: "We brushed out teeth together. I gave her the program for the day. We went to St. Peter's hospital to visit my father. He is on life support. When we got there the doctor told me there is nothing more they can do. He lost brain wave activity last night. I was told he is just existing, but he is not in there. I told the doctors that I needed to pray about it. I was unsure of what to do. The doctors assured me he is not going anywhere. I can take my time coming to a conclusion. They were very understanding. I take comfort in knowing that he isn't in any pain."

John said: "What is the name of this doctor?"

Alice said: "I think it was Dr. Mark Jacobs, but I am not clear on who he is right now."

John said: "We will look that up and interview him. What happened when you left the hospital?"

Alice said: "We went straight to St. Mark's church and then she disappeared into thin air."

John asked: "Does Jessica know about proper behavior in church?"

Alice siad: "She knows that when I tell her to sit next to me she will do it."

John asked: "Does she like to run around and tough everything and get nosy?"

Alice said: "She is rambunctious, but very obedient to my instructions. She is a little slow, so you have to explain everything."

John asked: "Does she go to Sunday Mass?"

Alice said: "St. Mark's is our parish. We go to Mass every Saturday night at 5:00. No matter what we plan we are always home by 5:00 Mass."

John asked: "Has anyone contacted you about a randsome?"

Alice said: "I haven't been home. I have been here."

7

JOHN RETURNED THE horse to the stables. It was his job to undress the horse every night. That meant take the saddle off and the muzzle, feed him, and water him. The saddle was to be hung up on a nail on the wall. He also had to clean the stall. All this work normally took about an hour. Since the horse liked him he had no trouble coming in there with the rake. John was instructed to report to Alice's house for further instructions. When he arrived he was told to sit down on the couch next to Alice. Shapiro had already bugged her phone. The idea was to monitor her phone and wait for a randome demand. After a week of monitoring her phone no randsome came in. John suggested that maybe the kidnapper is staying away because of that big crime scene bus right outside her door. He might be waiting for the bus to leave. That is a dead give away to a phone tap.

Detective Shapiro said: "John that is brilliant except for

one problem. He could have mailed in the randsome note. We have also been checking her mail. No randsome note as of yet."

John said: "That is my point. If we move the bus away he might think the cops gave up already."

Detective Shapiro said: "Joh, listen to what you just said. In most kidnappings the kidnapper doesn't want the child, just the money. What would he gain by keeping Jessica? He probably is laid off and has not money. How is he going to feed her every night? He just wants money probably to pay off his back rent until he can get a job and back on his feet again. My guess is tht she is unharmed being entertained by a TV

Or video. Most kidnappers want their victims to be as quiet as possible. He turned to Alice and asked: "Alice, what about her father?"

Alice said: "I have never been married. He told me he was visiting Las Vegas for the weekend. I think he spiked my drink. Then I turned up pregnant with Jessica. I never knew the guy's name. I never reported it because I was too embarrassed to admit it. I lived with the shame of having unprotected sex and sex before marriage. I tried to get right with God by having Jessica and keeping her. Father Raaser has always assured me that I did the right thing in the eyes of God. He assured me Jessica was put in my life for a reason. Now this happened."

Detective Shapiro asked: " How is it with just you and Jessica?"

Alice said: "Jessica has always been a slow child. When she was born she did not breath right away. She was without oxygen for 3 minutes. It was enough to slow down her development. Sometimes I lose patience with her when she is not getting what I am saying."

Detective Shapiro asked: "Is she exposed to other people such as family and friends?"

Alice said: "We are on our own out here. Both of my parents are dead. I had no siblings."

Detective Shapiro asked: "How many people know about the circumstances of Jessica's conception?"

Alice said: "Nobody knows the real truth. I tell people that her father was killed in Iraq. I pretend he was an army sergeant. It just seems easier that way."

Detective Shapiro asked: "What about a birth certificate?"

Alice said: "I put father unknown. The nurses said to was all right."

Detective Shapiro asked: "What hospital was Jessica born in?"

Alice said: "She was born in St. Peter's hospital. That is where I was born in and where we go for our medical needs. My father was brought there for his heart problems."

8

JOHN HAD THE bright idea to continually look for Jessica on horseback. He was leader of the team that searched the mountains of Nevada. On the other side was the colder weather. When nobody was looking he took something that had Jessica's scent on it and let the horse sniff her scent like a tracking dog. If anybody saw that he would have been laughed out of town. Shapiro wasn't surprised to hear that story. He dismissed it as just stupid locker room rumors. Every morning a team of ten policemen on horseback walked out to the woods to search for Jessica. They split up into teams of two in five different directions. After ten days of relentless searching Detective Shapiro called everyone together and came up with another tactic. He decided it was time for a news conference about this case. John's job was to organize it and gather everyone in one place.

9

THE NEXT DAY all the news people showed up at the church where the incident took place. Alice was there standing right next to Detective Shapiro. She was looking frail and at least ten pounds lighter. John was there to hold her up. Father Raaser was there also. They stood in front of the altar rail and explained the situation.

Detective Shapiro said: "Good morning everyone. Thank you for coming out this morning. I am holding this conference to ask your help with a problem we are having. The next person that takes my picture while I am speaking will be removed. You keep making me lose my thought. Back to the reason I am here. A week ago today Alice was a mother who came here to pray to god for guidance. Her five year old girl was with her and suddenly she was gone. She was wearing a red and white polka dot dress and matching sandals. We have searched evey nook and cranny from the raftors to the baseboards."

Father Raaser piped in and said: "Every morning I recheck everything from the raftors to the baseboards. We have rechecked the Baptismal Font and all the confessionals. I have to think like a five year old."

Detective Shapiro said: "One more thing I should say is that Jessica has the development of a 3 year old. She doesn't speak too much. She repeat the same words over and over again. She knows poty and cereal, not pronounced correctly. She is not developing at the appropriate rate of speed."

Detective Shapiro looked out on the crowd and was shocked to see Ronald Dennelly, an acquaintance from a previous case. Ronald stood up and requested permission to speak. Ronald said: "I might have some ideas on what you might be able to do with this search."

Detective Shapiro said: "Please meet me in the sacristy right after the news conference. I am open to any ideas you might have. He said to every one else if you have any information about this child please call the Las Vegas Police Department. All calls will be treated in the strictest of confidence. Thank you for coming everybody.

Somebody shouted: "What does the child look like? You only told us what she was wearing."

Detective Shapiro said: "Oh yeah. My apoligies for that mx up. She has blond hair, blue eyes and curly or wavy hair. Her body is the size of a four year old. Three feet five inches tall."

10

A T THE END Ronald and Sr. Angelus approached the altar. Ronald was pushing a baby carriage. The group adjourned to the sacristy. Dettective Shapiro introduced John the newest member on the team for this assignment. They chatted about John's background and make a little small talk.

Detective Shapiro said: "Ronald, wht was it you wanted to say?"

Ronald said: "OPkay. Father Raaser mentioned that he searches the church up and down every morning. What about the school next door?"

Sr. Angelus said: "Good question Ronald. This event occurred on a Saturday when the school was closed. All windows and doors are locked at 5:00 p.m. sharp. I have to get back to the convent in time for dinner and evening prayers. There is no way in creation a puny little five year old can fit through a closed window with metal bars screwed in."

Detective Shapiro said: "Okay. You both make good points. Let's do this. Tomorrow I will bring my team in to the school and we can search every nook and cranny in there. Call a lock down at 9:00 tomorrow. Every student in their seats until I give word that it is the all clear." Sr. Angelus told John to make sure Detective Shapiro is punctual. John assured her there will be him and nine other people. We will not touch or shake down the children for information.

11

THE NEXT DAY aat 8:45 sharp all members of the search party were in Sr. Angelus' office for a briefing. Even Detective Shapiro was there.

Sr. Angelus said: "My goodness Shapiro. You make it on time. How did yyou ever do that?"

Shapiro smiled and said: "John picked me up at 6:00 this morning. He took me to the diner for breakfast this morning. I had so much coffee I really nee dto use the restroom."

Sr. Angelus said: "Help yourself. Right arounbd the corner. Anyone else have to go?"

The other nine used the little boys room all at once. I was faster that way. When they reassembled in Sr. Angelus' office they were split up into two groups. Nobody was allowed to wander around the school unattended. Sr. Angelus, Detective Shapiro, and John were in one group and the rest were with Father Raaser. Sr. Angelus took the lower grades while Father Raaser took the upper grades. The first grade classroom was the first stop. When they entered a few students said good morning to Sr. Angelus.

Sr. Angelus said: "Good morning childfren. We have two visitors today to the school. They are on a special mission and they need your help to do it. Margaret stood up and shouted that she saw them on the news last night. She already knew they were police officers. Samuel jumped in and asked where they were talking from last night. John said: "We were in the church next door. The one that belongs to this parish."

Sam said: "Oh yeah. I thought that background looked familiar, but I couldn't place it. We'll be glad to help the police out. What can we do to help you?"

John asked: "Sam, where do you hang up your coats in the morning?"

Sam said: "In these closets here. Sr. Angelus calls them cubicles, but closet is easier to remember."

Detective Shapiro said: "Children, we have a plan. Please stand over by the window next to each othere. We will even let you watch us. If we do anything wrong we will have 25 witnesses to see it. They all got up and followed directions exactly. They were quiet, but very giggly watching the whole thing. John at first suggested that the children put their coats and hats on, but that was shot down by the teacher. The heat was still on because of the unusually cold weather. They methodically took out each and eery coat and shook it out. They checked all the arm sleeves of evey coat. Jophn said: Shapiro, think for a minute. Do you really

24

think a missing child could be hiding inside an arm sleeve of someone else's coat?"

Shapiro said: "I know it sounds crazy, but it worked for Stephanie Tanner on Full House." When they had finished every locker Shapiro asked the children to please put everything on top of the desk and empty it. They obliged gladly. When that was done the two detectives walked through the classroom and checked the inside of every desk. When they looked they realized everything was in the desk except for the kitchen sink. The teacher said it was atrocious to be that messy. The first graders spent the rest of the morning throwing out paper and making order. The same was done for the 2nd, 3rd, and kindergarten classes. Father Raaser's group did the same thing for the 4th through 8th grade classrooms. At the end the group reassembled outside the school office. They had one more task to do. They had to search the roof and boiler room of the school. John, Detective Shapiro and Sr. Angelus did that task. They even opened the boiler doors. John took out his flashlight and shined it between every pipe in the ceiling. This took longer than they expected. Their last stop was to search Sr. Angelus' office. That took no time flat because it was so small. Then they searched every inch of the secretary's office. She asked: "What are you looking for?"

Detective Shapiro said: "A missing child. He was down on all fours crawling on the floor looking underneath the desk."

Millie said:"Oh of course you are. Why didn't I think of that?" When they finished his final task was to announce the all clear signal that the lockown was over. The child was nowhere on the premisis."

12

WHEN THEY GOT outside John said the next step was to earch every hotel room on the strip. Steven said: "You're nuts John. It would take us a whole year to search every hotel room."

Detective Shapiro said: "Since you came up with it John, you are in charge. Where should we begin?"

John said: "Our first place will be the Liberace Museum. That encompasses two different buildings. We will all be together. Shapiro, Steven, you're with me. The rest of you will sweet talk the managers of the hotels. Start with the Burger King 2 doors down from the Motel Six where I work on the weekends. Start with the bathrooms and sweet talk your way into the kitchen. Don't do the dumpsters just yet. We will take 2 separate cars. Meet in Shapiro's office tomorrow morning at 9:00. Give a report on your findings and experiences. Good luck gentlemen. Use your badges if you need to.

When they arrived in the Liberace Museum there was a bus of tourists just pulling up. John, Steven, and Shapiro flashed their badges and asked to speak to the manager. Her name was Sally Connor. Luckily she was right there at the front desk. She asked: "Can I help you gentlemen?"

John said: "We need to call out a Code Adam. We are looking for a missing child in the area. Please line everybody up against the wall."

Sally said: "I recognized you two from TV last night. Visitor,ss please do as these cops ask. Everybody line up against the wall."

John said: "People, the sooner we do our job the sooner we can get out of your hair. I promise this won't take long. He turned to Sally and said: "We need to search both buldings. Every inch of the place. Lock all the doors and windows and show us to the exhibits."

Sally said: "Doors and windows are all locked. As soon as you mentioned Code Adam my assistant grabbed the keys and did that."

John said: "We need to search the trunk of every one of these cars. We will look in the windows an dtry not to disturb anything." Sally was reluctant, but she opened the trunks of every car in the museum. She had one master key. It only took 45 minutes because there was only about 10 cares to do. When they exhausted every hiding place possible they canceled the Code Adam and moved on the the next building. John thanked the tourists for their patience and wished them a happy stay in Las Vegas. Nobody minded the inconvenience. They readjusted the time of the tourist bus leaving to leave room for the show. Surprisingly nobody complained about the air conditioning. The only thing Sally insisted upon was that they wear cloth gloves so as not to disturb the old material in the cars. They gladly agreed to that. They moved on to the second building. The procedure was the same thing. The Code Adam. The locked doors only this time everybody was gathered in the Liberace Room where the shows were put on. At least this time the guests could sit down. Shapiro had to stop and ask questions about Liberace's home chapel. It was complete with Tabernacle, Altar, Monstronce with the Blessed Sacrament still exposed. The guide explained that because of his popularity people would be star struck and not give him any room to pray or pay attention to the Mass. He had a cousin come in every Satruday night at 5:00 to celebrate Mass for him. He was a Catholic Priest. The chapel is set up exactly as it was the morning he died. He simply went to Benediction and left us later on that day John woke him up and asked if he is ready to continue the search. They had to peek at the manicans to see if anyone was hiding in there. Shapiro and John were both in awe of the costumes. Sally finished giving them the tour and all were on their way. The cops thanked her for her help and cooperation and departed with a smile. Sally canceled the Code Adam and the museum reopened for business.

13

THE NEXT DAY all parties of the search team met in the parking lot because Shapiro did not have enough chairs for everyone.

John asked: "How did your search go yesterday?"

Mark said: "It went very well surprisingly. We ran into no resistance at all. The manager of Burger King let us into the bathrooms and the kitchen. You have no idea how many blond haired blue eyed girls use that play area. The manager asked that all children return to their parents. All the children wre claimed by an adult. The manager then took us into the kitchen area. All emplyees lined up against one wall and we searched the closets and food pantries. Nothing was there. We thanked the manager and moved on to the Motel Six. The manager there saw you on the news last night. He searched every room and bathroom last night. He allowed us to search every room again. He came with us. We turned all the beds upside down. Nothing was found.

I did find $1.50 in dropped change, but no lost children. What is our next move?"

John said: "Our next move is to search every hotel room on the strip. "

Shapiro said: "Please tell me he didn't just say that."

Mark said: "John, have you totally gone off your rocker? That is at least twenty hotels and motels and God only knows how many rooms."

John said: "Not if we do this in teams. Me, Shapiro, and Steven will start with the Flamingo Hotel. The rest of you will do the Bellagio. That encompasses at least 2 different buildings. Have the managers call out a Code Adam on the PA systems as you search. It will not be as daunting as it sounds. I promise. Trust me."

Shapiro said: "You heard the man. You have your assignments. Let's move it out. Meet back here on Monday morning for a report on your findings. " They al departed for the weekend. When they got to the Flamingo the manager came right away to see them. John gave his story as to why they were there. The manager got on the PA system and called out the Code Adam. Their first stop was the side entrance where the tours left from. Security was posted at the door to lock and unlock the door as the buses arrived. When all the tours left for the day the door was locked for good. At the end of the day the same routine was followed for the arrivals back home. It ood until 8:00 to search every hotel room and every hiding spot there could be. The tricky part was the arrival of the guests. They were leaving and coming in all day. Shapiro thanked the manager at the end for his cooperation. The manager promised to keep in touch.

14

THE GROUP ADJOURNED for the evening and reunited the next morning in the station house. John gave his report about there experience trying to search the Flamingo hotel. Mark talked about trying to search every inch of the Bellagio. That was a nightmare because of the mall inside the hotel. It took them until midnight to finish that one. The managers of both hotels were only too happy to search their hotel. They did make progress in that they agreed to pin up Jessica's picture on all the public areas of the hotel. It will be done by morning.

Their meeting was interrupted by Shapiro's secretary who entered with a stack of at least 600 messages all stating that they have seen Jessica. She has been seen everywhere from an Air Lingus airplane to New York and Florida. It was the job of the team to ferret out the legitimate sitings from the illegitimate ones. Luckily the cops knew information that was net released. One was from a specific psychic who has an uncanny ability to be right. About 10:00 that morning Alice showed up at Shapiro's office for an update on the investigation. Alice had a picture of Jessica in her purse. Shapiro asked if she had any birthmarks or things on her body. She hadn't remembered any new scars on her body.

John asked: "Shapiro, what do you make of this specific message?"

Shapiro said: " Don't trust that one. That psychic is not for real. She came out with information that killed her credibility. She has called the station n other crimes. When she was questioned she had connections to the Lord God of Hosts, The Holy Spirit, and the Holy Ghost. She even called the cops and claimed that Jesus Christ was walking around her garden. That turned out to be the gardener next door."

John said: "You did say follow the leads."

Shapiro said: "Wrong. You told us to sift throught he messages and pick out the legitimate ones. If you insist on following this go ahead. Just don't tell me I didn't warn you."

15

JOHN TOOK A trip to the psychic's house just over the mountains. When he rang the bell the door was opened by an overweight woman named Jenna. He said: "Good morning madam. I am with the Las Vegas Police Department. I understand you had a sighting of a missing child named Jessica."

Jenna said: "Well it is about time you got to me. I have proof that the kid is still alive and well." She put a video tape into the VCR and pushed play. On the screen came a group of children playing outside in a backyard. John watched the tape and after two minutes saw Jessica on the screen wearing the same clothes she was wearing the day she disappeared. John almost fell out of the chair. He said: "Jenna, where di dyou get this tape?"

Jenna said: "I was visiting a friend in Ely, Nevada and she came out. My friend said it was an elderly woman and her son Baxter. Jenna appeared on March 18th. They never go to school. The woman is very sickly and can't live alone. The children are there to take care of her.

John asked: "How many children are there?"

Jenna said: "It is hard to tell. They seem to come and go."

John said: "I need to take this tape with me. I also need the exact address of this location." He burst into Shaprio's office with the tape and started screaming about his find. Shapiro watched the tape and almost fell out of his chair. He asked: "Who are these other kids?"

John said: "Jenna didn't know."

Shapiro said: "Gather the team. We have a trip to make. It takes about 90 minutes to get there from here. I will alert Ely police department and alert them of the situation." They took three police cars and sped down the highway as fast as was safe. As long as they were blowing the sirens people had not problem m=oving over and letting them pass. Their first stop was the Ely police department to bring in local witnesses. The deputy recognized whose yard it was as soon as he saw the tape. He knew Baxter was fairly new in town and that his mother was very sickly. Baxter always presented himself as a hard worker, but not sociable at all. They all adjourned to the house, the local deputy in the lead. They were able to walk to the house. The door was opened after the third knock. John was ready to pull out his gun, but Shapiro corrected him just in time. The door was opened by a fat out of shape woman who could barely walk. She walked with a cane and had very swollen legs that barely carried her. She sherrif asked: "Where is Baxter?"

The woman said: "He is working. He will be back at 5:00 tonight."

John screamed: "WHERE IS BAXTER? Who are all these kids?"

The woman screamed: "These kids help take care of me. I can't be left alone. We can't afford a nursing home. Baxter says these kids are street kids. He says nobody will miss them. He is doing them a favor by taking them in and keeping them off the streets!!!"

John said: "Give me Jessica." The Ely sherriff's office took the other nine children and interviewd them individually. It was discovered that they were all missing children. One was from Salt Lake City, Utah. The others were more local residents. They were all taken to the hospital for medical exams. They were found to be healthy except for a vitamin deficiency because of a lack of sunlight. They were allowed a phone call to their parents and were returned home in a police car. They had to keep a record of all the addresses and phone numbers. All the parents agreed to let them testify at the trial to put him away for life. Steven made his first arrest when he arrested Baxter for kidnapping. He protested that his crimes took place elsewhere. Steven said: "Too bad. You have a right to remain silent. Anything you say can and will be used against you in a court of law. You have the right to an attorney. If you cannot afford one one will be provided for you. Do you understand these gihts as I have explained them to you?"

Baxter said: "Yes I do."

Steven said: "Bearing these rights in midn do you wish to talk to me at this time?"

Baxter said: "No. I prefer not to speak at this time. John sat in the back seat with Jessica. Detective Shapiro drove at a leisurely pace. He wanted Jessica and John to do a little sightseeing. They couldn't see much from the highway. The Ely Police Department escorted themm as far as the county line. Jessica waved good bye to the other officers. They strobe lights started to bother Jessica after a while. They arrived home around 1:00 a.m. Detective Shapiro explained that Jessica had a medical exam and was found to be health except for a vitamin deficiency because of a lack of sunlight. For tonight all shee needs is mild and cookies and bed. Shapiro and John crashed in Alice's house for the night because it was too late to drive home.

16

Baxter's attorney was named Gene O'Dowd. First thing in the morning Baxter met Gene and they came up with a defense strategy. He was scheduled to stand trial Jan. 5th. He was ordered helf without bail. He pleaded not guilty to the charge of kidnapping. The judge assigned to the case was Judge Michael McClintock. He was a no nonsense judge who would not tolerate outbursts or inappropriate behavior. Everybody was on their best behavior. Trial always started exactly on time. Baxter was led into the court room in handcuffs and leg irons. He was warned beforehand about proper behavior.

The prosecuting attorney opened with the statement of the video tape of the children. The defense attorney opened with the statement that the children went with him willingly. The prosecuting attorney's name was Elizabeth Dunn.

Michael said: "Elizabeth, call your first witness."

Elizabeth said: "I call John Reyes to the stand. When John approached he was sworn in. The bailiff said: " Do you solemnly swear to tell the truth the whole truth and nothing but the truth so help you God?"

John said: "I do." He took his seat.

Elizabeth said: "John, pleae tell the court your job."

John said: "I am antually a mounted police officer. My job is to take care of the horse in the stable and the horse's hygiene. The only thing I don't do is take care of the feet and teeth. A furrier is called in to do that. I hav eto fee, water, and clean the horse.

Elizabeth asked: "How did you come about getting involved in the case?"

John said: "This case started on St. Patrick's day. I was on call for security for the parade when the call came in about a problem in St. Mark's Church. As soon as the horse heard that I swear he took off like a rocket. The horse rememberd being there for a carnival."

Elizabeth asked: "What did you find when you got there?"

John said: "I had to open the doors and the horse trotted up the center aisle and knelt at the Communion Rail." There were giggled all around the court room for that one.

Elizabeth said: "Please continue. What else did you see?"

John said: "I did see one lady and a uniformed officer sitting in the back row. I didn't notice her right away. I was too busy trying to control the horse. Nobody was up front at the time. Then I saw Detective Shapiro and the pastor father Raaser come out of the sacristy. Father Raaser started to make goo-goo noises and tickle the horse under its chin. Detective Shapiro saw the horse and went ballistic. He asked who called the mounted police. He ordered me to dismount. He screamed at Raaser to focus. I was tolk to take the lady home and sit with her. We waited a whole week for a ransome demand to come in. When none came we switched tactics. We got a thousand calls stating that the girl was seen everywhere from Florida to Texas and even one to an Aer Lingus flight going to Ireland. Then I checkd out a call from a psychic who said she was in Ely, Nevada. Shapiro told me to forget about that one because she has seen the Lord God of Hosts, the Holy Ghost, and the Holy Spirt as well as Jesus Christ in her garden. That turned out to be the gardener next door. He said go ahead and check it out if I insist on wasting my time. I did."

Elizabeth asked: "What did you find when you got there?"

John said: "The house was immaculate. The flower beds were well arranged. The inside f the house was also immaculate. There was a tea set for show on the coffee table. She wasn't the most polite person to talk to though. When I saw here she said it was about time I showed up. Then she showed me a video tape of her friends in Ely, Nevada. The children were in the house next door. They rarely came out."

Elizabeth asked: "When did you approach the defendant?"

John saie: "I approached the next day. I had to report it to Detective Shapiro first. He came up with a plan that was fool proof. We didn't want to warn him first so he would ave a chance to dump the kids somewhere else. We left at six o'clock in the morning and put on the lights and sirens all the way up there. Itw as at least a six hour ride without traffic. When we came blaring through the traffic was glad to move over and let us pass. That saved us some time. We arrived at approximately 12:00 noon. We stopped off at the sherriff's office first to have a presence for local law enforcement. They were there for backup. We didn't want him to run."

Elizabeth asked: "Were they cooperative with your theory?"

John said: We showed him the videotape of the children and some were recognized immediately. We had their full cooperation right from the start."

Elizabeth said: "Thank you John. No more questions."

The judge said: "Gene, do you have any questions?"

Gene said: "Not at this time your honor. We reserve the right to recall this witness at a later time in the trial."

The judge said: "You may step down John."

17

DAY TWO OF the trial started at 8:30 in the morning in the judge's chambers. He wanted a report of the game plan for the trial. Elizabeth said they were going to interview the children that were kidnapped. They were going to start out with the sherriff of Ely, Nevada and then move on to the parents and the childen. They adjourned to the court room and the bailiff yelled ALL RISE!!!"

The judge said: "Elizabeth, you may begin when ready."

Elizabeth said: "I call the Sherriff of Ely, Nevada." As the sherriff approached he was sworn in to tell the truth the whole truth and nothing but the truth."

Elizabeth asked: "How do you know the defendant?"

The sherriff said: "He is fairly new in the town of Ely, Nevada. He is not very friendly at all. He never smils or chit chats with anyone. If you ask him a question his answers are short an in a way that doesn't invite further conversation."

Elizabeth asked: "How do the people treat him in the stores?"

The sherriff said: "We give him whatever he wants and we give him the same expressionless attitude he gives us. It seems to work."

Elizabeth said: "Thank you. No more questions your honor."

The judge said: "Gene, do you have any questions for this witness?"

Gene said: "Thank you your honor. Now sherriff, isn't it true that Baxter tried to talk to your officers?"

The sherriff said: "I am not aware of Baxter ever talking to anyone."

Gene asked: "Isn't it ture that Baxter patronizes the stores in town?"

The sherriff said: "Yes. I have seen him in the Quickie Mart gas station. He was buying gas for his car."

Gene asked: "Has he been seen in the company of his mother?"

The sherriff said: "He has always been seen alone. I knew he lived with her, but they were never together"

Gene asked: "How did you know they were living together?"

The sherriff said: "I drove by their house and saw her sitting on the porch in a rocking chair. I walked over and introduced myself. I just wanted to let her know who I was and that she can call me if she needs anything."

Gene asked: "What was her reaction to you coming up on her porch like that?"

The sheriff said: "She greeted me with anger in her eyes. Baxter came up behind me just then. He thanked me for my concern and I was abruptly dismissed. I asked him if she had a previous stroke and he said yes. He asked me why I would care about that. I said because I am the sheriff and if something happens to her I would be able to tell the paramedics about it."

Gene asked: "Where did Baxter work in town?"

The sheriff said: "Baxter worked in the wood factory. He made bunk beds for people to sell. He was very good at it too.

Gene said: "No more questions your honor."

The judge said: "You may step down. And sheriff, don't forget your firearm when you leave the courthouse."

18

AFTER LUNCH WHEN everybody returned the judge instructed Elizabeth to call her first witness.

Elizabeth said: "I call Margaret McDonough to the stand." As Margaret approached two people went to the stand. Elizabeth smiled and said Margaret senior. Little Margaret laughed and said: "Sorry madam. I was named after my mother. The judge said to little Margaret that she will have her turn when her mother finishes testifying. Little Margaret took her seat at the prosecution table. It was the first seat she saw. Everybody smiled at her excitement and innocence. The judge was very impressed with her obedience and proper behavior in court.

Elizabeth said: "Now big Margaret please tell us about the morning little Margaret disappeared."

Margaret said: "I took her to the playground when she was four years old. We were playing hide and seek. We kept running around the play things. We got to this big thing that the kids climb on. It resembled a house of sorts. I was on one side on the inside and she was on the outside. When I flipped around she was gone. It was as though she vanished into thin air."

Elizabeth asked: "What did you do when you discovered this?"

Margaret said: "I looked around and discovered that I was the only one in the playground. There was literally no place else to hide. It was an open playground. I called the police right away. We called every one of her friends. I called all of my friends. Ait was a small town, so strange people and cars would stand out like a soar thumb. Nobody reported seeing anything of the sort. The sherriff even organized a door to door search of every house in town. We had one hopeful breakthrough. The sherriff showed the picture to one family. They showed it to their beagle dog and the dog started wagging its tail furiously. They took the dog for a walk with the instruction to show us where the child was seen. The dog led them straight to the playground, which was the last place she was seen. The dog was given the scent of Margaret an the dog retraced every step Margaret and I made. He lost the scent at the corner, which told us she was probably stuffed into a car."

Gene said: "Objection your honor!!! Are you gonna tell us the dog found the missing child?"

The judge said: "Overruled. If you were listening Gene you would have heard the dog came up with the idea that she went into a car. Start listening to the witnessess!!!"

Elizabeth asked: "How long was the search for your daughter?"

Margaret said: "About a month I think. At that point another child was stolen and the sherriff said he had to start looking for someone else. He promised me that he would not give up."

Elizabeth asked: "What did you do at that point?"

Margaret said: "At that point I tried to make the most of the situation. I went over to the house of the next missing child. His name was Matthew O'Donnell. I went to sit with the hysterical mother. I held her hand and we worried about him. We put our heads together and tried to make sense of it. The sherriff said that we needed to write down everything the two children have in common."

Elizabeth asked: "Did you come up with anything they had in common?"

Margaret said: "Yes, several things. They both had blond hair and brown eyes, they are both in the first grade, and they both go to the same school. People often mistook them for twins."

Elizabeth asked: "Did anyone think mybe the wrong child was taken?"

Margaret said: "The sheriff suggested that, but I never dwelt on that point."

Elizabeth asked: "How long was Margaret missing?"

Margaret said: "She was missing for two years. The sherriff always said to keep the faith and that I should never give up. He always believed that Margaret was alive somewhere."

Elizabeth said: "Thank you Margaret. No more questions your honor."

The judge said: "Call your next witness Gene."

Gene got up and said: "I call Margaret Junior to the stand."

Little Margaret got up and took the stand. She was very excited to sit up there. She looked all around wide eyed and fascinated. The judge smiled at her and made her feel relaxed and focused.

Gene said: "Do you know the defendant?"

Margaret asked the judge: "Sorry judge. Which one is the defendant?"

Gene said: "That man sitting in that chair. Do you know him?"

Margaret said: "Yes sir. He stole me from the playground. Then she said to the judge:" Is it all right if Elizabeth asks me the questions? Gene is scaring me."

The judge said: "Of course Margaret. We want you to be as comfortable and relaxed as possible. Gene, please be seated and do not look at Margaret. Elizabeth, please take over the questioning and remember this is a six year old child. Be gentle and respectful."

Elizabeth asked: "How long were you living with Baxter, that man over there?"

Margaret said: "Two years I lived with him. He was always strict with us doing our chores and doing everything we were told. There were consequences for not doing what we were told/"

Elizabeth asked: " What was the punishment for not doing what you were told?"

Margaret said: "He would hit us a lot. I wet myself a lot, so he switched to locking me in the basement."

Elizabeth asked: "How long were you in the basement?"

Margaret said: "I don't know. I still can't tell time. He had no clocks in his house. Then one day he surprised me with Matthew O'Donnell. He was a friend from kindergarten. I still remembered him. Eventually he brought in the other kids."

Elizabeth asked: "What about the phones in the house?"

Margaret said: "There were no phones in the house. I can only assume he had a cell phone in his pocket. We were not allowed in his room. Once kid went in there and was caught. He skinned her alive for five minutes straight. She walked funny and couldn't sit down for a week. She had to sleep on her stomach for a week. After lights out at night we put powder on her tussie. We saw the bruises. Matthew found some ointment of sorts and put that on her."

Elizabeth asked: "What did you do during the day?"

Margaret said: "We had to help out his mother. The old lady in the house."

Elizabeth asked: "How did you help her out?"

Margaret said: "We had to pull up her zipper on her dress, tie her shoes, put her socks on, and snap her bra into place. This was all too hard for me because I didn't understand any of it. She hit me with her cane."

Elizabeth asked: "When did you play"

Margaret said: "We played maybe once a week and that was only if the house was spotless."

Elizabeth said: "Thank you Margaret. No more questions your honor."

The judge said: "Thank you Margaret. You were very brave. He is an apple juice as a reward for doing this."

Margaret said: "Thank you judge."

The judge said: "You may step down Margaret. Elizabeth, call your next witness please."

Gene said: "Pardon me judge. I beliebe it is my turn."

The judge said: "My apologies Gene. Elizabeth, please be seated and wait."

Elizabeth said: "Gladly your honor."

Gene said: " I call Matthew O'Donnell."

Matthew approached the stand and was sworn in. The bailiff said: "Do you solemnly swear to tell the truth the whole truth and nothing but the truth so help you God?"

Matthew said: "I do."

Gene said: "Now Matthew please tell us about the abduction."

Matthew said: "I was abducted on the bus stop. I was waiting for my school bus."

Gene asked: "Why didn't you run away?"

Matthew said: "Nobody was there. I was early for the us."

Gene asked: "Didn't you rscream or run away?"

Matthew said: "He grabbed me out of nowhere. He upt his hand on my mout and shoved me into the car."

Gene asked: "Didn't you have that talk with your parents?"

Matthew screamed: "I was six years old. I did the best I could."

The judge said: "Enough Gene. He said he was six years old. Your questioning is finished. Take your seat and don't speak to this witness again." Then he said to Elizabeth: "Elizabeth, take over the questioning."

Elizabeth said: "Thank you your honor. Now Matthew, please tell us about the day you disappeared."

Matthew said: "As I said we were on the bus stop. I did hear a lot of people screaming that there was a kidnapping in progress. I guess there were witnesses after all."

Elizabeth asked: "Where were you taken to?"

Matthew said: "When I was thrown into the car I was knocked on the head. When I came to there was a blanket thrown over my head. I couldn't see anything. We drove for a long time. Finally we stopped and he pulled me into the house."

Elizabeth asked: "What time was it that you stopped?"

Matthew said: "I think the sun was setting. I didn't know north, south, east and west. If I could have known that I could have figured out what time it was. One thing I do remember is there were shadows in front of me, so I am guessing it was sometime in the afternoon."

Elizabeth asked: "How did he treat you in the beginning?"

Matthew said: "He threw me into a chair and closed the blinds. He let me know right from the start that he was to be obeyed. I believe him to be very much micro aggressive."

Gene said: "Objection your honor. Move to strike this child's whole testimony."

The judge said: "Now what is your problem?"

Gene said: "How on earth is this child supposed to

know the word microggressive? I barely know what that means. He has obviously been coached which is a direct violation of the order of the court signed by you judge!!!"

Matthew said: "It means genius that he saw me as a kid so he automatically talked to me like an idiot. The summer before I was kidnapped my abysitter was a teenager. She spent the whole day on the phone and listening to the walkman. I could have been dancing in the nude naked on top of the kitchen table with angel wings on. She wouldn't have noticed. I ended up reading a dictionary. When I finished I read the beginning and learned about prefixes and suffixes."

The judge said: "Now Matthew did anybody tell you what to say?"

Matthew said: "My mother nad Detective Shapiro just said to tell the truth no matter what it soulds like. She said not to worry about the cursing."

The judge said: "Gene, your objection is overruled. Continue Elizabeth."

Elizabeth asked: "How did he treat Jessica?"

Matthew said: "Jessica was ht in the knees with the can a lot. She didn't talk much, but she didn't have household skills either. She was like a baby. My job was to show her how to do the household chores. She used the potty a lot, which made Baxter mad. She was the first to go to bed. She nexter asked what time it was."

Elizabeth asked: "Did you guys sleep all night?"

Matthew said: "No. I got up at least twice a night. I went to the bathroom and sometimes stayed up. The other kids usually got up around the same time."

Elizabeth asked: "Did he touch you inappropriately?"

Matthew said: "He tried, but I hit him in the mouth, cheek, and elbowed him in the eye. He never touched me like that again."

Elizabeth asked: "Did he touch the other kids inappropriately?"

Matthew said: "If he edid they never talked about it. You will have to ask them about that. We were between the ages of five and seven, so we probably didn't know any better."

Elizabeth said: "Thank you Matthew. No more questions your honor."

The judge said: "Gene, do you have any questions?"

Gene said: "Matthew, why did you get into the car?"

Matthew said: "I already told you he snatched me off the corner."

Gene asked: "Were you the oldest child?"

Matthew said: "I don't know. We never talked about that."

Gene asked: "Why didn't you escape at night?"

Matthew said: "They had a dead bolt on both doors and an alarm on the kitchen door. They also had an alarm on all the windows. One of the kids tried to open the windows. She was beaten to a pulp. She never head of an alarm on a window."

Gene asked: "Who was this that tried to escape?"

Matthew said: "I don't remember I am foggy on names."

Gene said: "No more questions your honor."

The judge gave Matthew an apple juice and a pack

of cookies. He said: "Thank you Matthew. You may step down." The judge announced that they are finished for the day. Eveyrbody was to return by 9:00 the next morning."

19

THE NEXT MORNING started in the judge's chambers. He wanted a report on the progress of the trial. Both lawyers agreed to finish within the next five days. The jdge warned Geneto hold his tongue and not be disruptive during court. He promised to behave himself. They adjourned at 9:00 sharp. The judge said: "Elizabeth, call your first witness."

Elizabeth said: "I call Alice Donaghue to the stand." As Alice approached the stand she was sworn in by the bailiff.

Elizabeth said: "alice, please tell us about the day Jessica disappeared."

Alice said: "It was St. Patrick's day. I woke up and woke Jessica. We went through the usual morning routine. Nothing seemed amiss about Jessica."

Elizabeth asked: "How old was Jessica at the time?"

Alice said: "She was five, but had the development of a

three year old. She was also the height of a three year old. She didn't speak too much."

Elizabeth asked: "What did the pediatritican say about that?"

Alice said: "He said not to worry about it. She was just a late bloomer."

Elizabeth asked: "Do you always to to church in the middle of the week?"

Alice said: "No. That was a special occasion. We normally go to church on Saturday night. That was our special time. No matter where we went we found a church tht had Mass at 5:00. Jessica didn't know the days of the week, but somehow she always knew when it was Saturday."

Elizabeth asked: "Was she in school?"

Alice said: "No. She was rejected because she failed the admissions test. I was told to put her in therapy and get her caught up. It wasn't working."

Elizabeth asked: "What brought you to the church that morning?"

Alice said: "I was there to pray for guidance. When we went to the hispital to visit my father we were told to decide whether or not to take him off of life support. He had a massive stroke ad was not expected to make it.

Elizabeth asked; "Did your father make it?"

Alice said: "We came to a compromise with the doctors. I felt justified in taking him off life support provided I donated his organs. His live, eyes, stomach, and intestines were donated. Five people got a second chance of life because of him. Four people were cancer patients. I have no knowledge of who they are. His eyes were sent to Cambodia where a lot of children are going blind for no fault of their own."

Elizabeth asked: "What was your reaction to Jessica vanishing?"

Alice said: "I was mortified and panicked right away. I started screaming and running around. Father Raaser came running out of the sacristy to check on me. He called 911 from his cell phone. Then the whole incident took off from there. I remember a horse running up the aisle, but I thought I was hallucinating. I still can't picture what the horse was doing there."

Elizabeth asked: "How long was Jessica missing?"

Alice said: "Maybe nine months, maybe eight months. I am not sure. I do know it wasn't quite a year yet."

Elizabeth asked: "What was your reaction when you found her?"

Alice said: "I turned white and lost my balance. Somehow I always knew she was out there somewhere. She wasn't too smart and had the mind of a three year old. Detective Shapiro drove her home in his police car. She asked for the lights and sirens."

Elizabeth asked: "What is her condition now?"

Alice said: "She is caut up and is functioning at a six year old level. Detective Shapiro said she was never sexually molested. She was examined at the hospital before I was called. Her only problem is she has long periods of silence. She apparently has an interest in flowers. I don't know where that came from. She is also very helpful around the house."

Elizabeth said: "Thank you Alice. No more questions your honor."

The judge said: "Gene, you may begin when ready."

Gene said: "Now Alice, you testified that you went to the church to pray for guidance."

Alice said: "That's right."

Gene said: "If you knew your child was slow why was she left unsupervised?"

The judsgc yelled: "QUIT BEING A POMPUS HEINEY HOLE!!! I say that out of respect for the ladies and the children in the court room."

Gene asked: "Does she talk about her days in captivity?"

Alice said "Once in a while she will slip out a sentence or two. Not too often."

Gene asked: "Is she in school now?"

Alice said: "Yes. She goes to second grad eand first grade on Saturdays. Sr. Angelus hired a tutor for her to catch up."

Gene asked: "Have you ever met the defendant before?"

Alice said: "No. We have never met."

Gene said: "Of course not. After all, you weren't paying attention to who was around you."

The dudge said: "Enough Gene!!! I have had it with your smart remarks!! One more time and you will be held in contempt.!!!"

Gene said: "My apoligies your honor."

The jduge said: "Turn around and face the court and apologize fror your behavior."

Gene had no choice but to follow instructions from the judge."

The judge said: " Elizabeth, call your next witness please."

Elizabeth said: "I call Jessica to the stand." As Jessica approached the stand she was sworn in by the bailiff.

When Jessica was seated Elizabeth said: "Good morning Jessica."

Jessica said: "Good morning Elizabeth. Good morning judge."

The judge smiled and said: "Good morning Jessica. All you have to do today is tell us the truth about wht happened. If you don't understand or are uncomfortable, just tell us and we will move on to another question."

Jessica said: "He is not gonna bother me again?"

The judge said: "I give you my word he will never bother you again."

Jessica said: "Okay judge. I'm ready Elizabeth."

Elizabeth smiled and said: "Now Jessica, do you remember when you were taken from the church?"

Jessica said: "Yes. Mommy was praying and I was just sitting there. She said Father Raaser had a present for me in the Baptismal Font. He called it the water fountain. There was a gift box in there. It had my name on it. When I opened the package it was a doll. He said Father Raaser wanted to play hide and seek. He put me in a paper sack and carried me into a car. I would go to my death for Father Raaser. I liked him. He was nice to me. He didn't treat me like an idiot."

Elizabeth asked: "When did you first realize you were being taken?"

Jessica said: "When I felt us move I was watching out the window. I screamed a lot, but he cover me up again and wouldn't let me be heard. There was a window above me, but all I saw was the blue sky. I had the doll with me, so I pretended it was the angels looking after me."

Elizabeth asked: "Where did you learn about angels?"

Jessica said: "I learned that from Father Raaser. We used to talk in the sacristy."

Elizabeth asked: "Did Father Raaser teach you when you were alone?"

Jessica said: "No. There were always altar boys and nuns around."

Elizabeth asked: "When were these lessons with Father Raaser?"

Jessica said: "I don't know."

Elizabeth asked: "Was it before you disappeard or after?"

Jessica said: "Before I disappeared."

Elizabeth asked: "What happened when you arrived at his house?" She pointes to the defendant.

Jessica said: "That is when I knew I was in trouble. He threw me into a chair and laid down the law. He gave me the run down on the rules of the house. I was to do the dishes and clean the house."

Elizabeth asked: "Did he hit you?"

Jessica said: "Yes he hit me a lot. He hurt me on my sit upon."

Elizabeth asked: "You seem to be very vocal. When did you develop this speech ability?"

Jessica said: "I might have known all along, but I probably chose not to. I don't know why."

Elizabeth asked: "Did he ever touch you inappropriately?"

Jessica said: "No. There was none of that."

Elizabeth said: "Thank you Jessica. No more questions your honor."

The judge said: "Gene, do you have any questions for this witness?"

Gene said: "Yes your honor. Now Jessica, why did you not sit where you were told?"

Jessica said: "I don't remember. Maybe I was distracted. Somebody tell me they hava e apresent for me I would have gone."

Gene asked: "Are you always disobedient to your mother?"

Elizabeth said: "Objection your honor!!! She already answered that question."

The judge said: "Sustained. Jessica, you can ignore the question. No need to answer that one. The judge gave her an apple juice and a pack of cookies. He told her she may step down.

20

THE LAST DAY of the trial started with the judge giving instructions to the jury about the charges. The charges were four counts of attempted kidnapping and endangering the welfare of a child four counts. The sentence to be imposed is twenty five years to life or the death penalty. First they will hear closing arguments from the lawyers and the prosecution. "Elizabeth, you may begin when ready."

Elizabeth got up and said: "Thank you your honor. Ladies and gentlemen of the jury. Baxter was a man who was in a quandary. He claims he didn't mean no harm, but I doubt that. He wanted his mother to have help, but he couldn't afford a nursing home. He could have applied for adult day care centers. But he chose the route of kidnapping. What right does he have to use children to do the job of grown ups. He could have taken the time to teach them what he wants instead of beathing them black and blue. You musst find him guilty on all counts."

21

WHEN IT WAS his turn Gene got up with his closing argument. He said: "Ladies and gentlement of the jury. Baxter is innocent of all kidnapping charges because he never asked for a ransome note. There is no question that he took them, but the parents are to blame for this because all of the kids were unsupervised in a public place. If the parents cared about the kids they would have kept a better eye on them. He did beat them black and blue because the parents failed to teach them right from wrong."

The judge almost fell off his chair when he heard that. He couldn't wait to leave. He had to restrain himself from screaming at Gene for a remark like that. The jury was instructed not touse personal feelings when judging if Baxter is guilty or not. Just use the facts as presented. When he finally did get back to his office he sat down with Elizabeth and came down with a case of diarrhea of the mouth. They were both incensed that anybody would even write such ideas.

22

THE JURY ASKED for read backs of several testimonies. After two weeks of constant negotiating the jury decided they were deadlocked. There was no way they could agree on guilt or not. They never even got to the penalty phase. The vote was six against six. The judge had no choice but to dismiss the charges against Baxter and release him back into society.

23

ONE YEAR AFTER Baxter's release sure enough he was at it again. The missing child in Ely, Nevada. This time the sherriff searched his house first. His mother died one month after his dismissal. When the sherriff broke in he heard a scream from the basement. He kicked the door down and rescued the little girl. She somehow remembered the self defense SING. Eyesockets, Instep, Nose, Groin. Even though she was only seven years old she paid attention in gym class. She kept her wits enough to remember that. After Baxter was exposed all the children in town were taught self defense. The sherriff arrested him on the spot. He second trial ended with a conviction. He was sent to jail for life. His home was sold to a new town member who was new to the state of Nevada. They managed to pay for it in one lump sum. The money was used to pay for the training of the next class of cops. Poor Baxter couldn't even stand up straight.

24

ONE YEAR AFTER baxter's conviction he was stabbed to death in the showers with a shank. It was instant death because he was stabbed straight in the heart. There was a funeral at the prison and a burial next door, but there were no tears shed for this prisoner. Everybody tried to get their hands on him since the day he arrived. His crimes proved why he should be the most hated man there was. Over the course of the year he was framed for drugs in his cell. He was sent to isolation for two weeks. The prisoners thought that was crueal punishment and matched his horrendous crimes. This was done by other prisoners who were already in there for life. The warden looked the other way. The guards also looked the other way. They never ratted out who was behind the set up of the drugs.

25

D ETECTIVE SHAPIRO MADE a call to the prison out of the blue. He wanted to know exactly what the prisons are doing to reform people, not just punish them. The warden explained that at her prison they have a new program called boot camp. So far there have been no return of prisoners for other crimes of those who have taken it. Baxter actually flunked out of the program. He was accused of nonparticipating in activities. The drill seargeants decided he was a liability to the program, so he was returned to general population. She personally observed him being the outcast of not participating.

26

EVEN THOUGH BAXTER was put to death Gene couldn't shake the feeling that something was missed in the trial of Baxter. He went to the court house and asked for the evidence box for Baxter's trial. He looked at the tape over and over again until his eyeballs wanted to fall out. He finally noticed something new. The tape showed the man with a birthmark near his eye. He never noticed that on Baxter himself. He had to take a trip to Ely and visit his home again. He found a strange man sunning himself on the lawn. He asked: "What is your name?"

The man said: "My name is Lucas. This is my house. I grew up here. I have been out in school abroad for a year. Where is my mother?"

Gene said: "I am sorry. Your mother died a month after the trial and your brother was put to death for kidnapping."

Lucas asked: "When did this happen?"

Gene said: "He was put to death maybe about six months ago."

Lucas asked: "What brings you back here?"

Gene said: "I can't shake the feeling that something was missed at the trial. By the way, how did you get that scar on your forehead?"

Lucas said: "I got it from a fall when I was a child. I probably fell in the playground or something. I had stitches put in, but my exact injury is no longer in my mind. I never focus on that scar."

Gene asked: "How long will you be in town?"

Lucas said: "I am here to stay. I am not going anywhere. My mother let us know that when she dies she wanted me to have the house. My brother gets it first and then I do."

27

At that point the sherriff pulled up and got out of his car. He asked Lucas who he was and why was he trespassing on someone else's property?"

Lucas explained that he was the survivor of the family of Baxter. The sherriff said the house was sold to another couple and that they were on vacation. He no longer had any claim to the house. He really needed to leave the premisis. Lucas left, but Gene wanted to get a word privately with the sherriff. He showed him the tape and there was no scar on Baxter's forehead. Lucas claimed he had stitches as a child. The sherriff said he will investigate, but it is too late to bring Baxter back. What is done is done.

28

THE SHERRIFF'S FIRST stop was to go back to the prison and get a picture of him on his first day of admission. There was no scar on Baxter's forehead, which told them that Lucas was the real kidnapper. On the tape the guy had the scar. The sherriff's first step was to call Detective Shapiro for advice. He wasn't sure what to do first or what to make of it.

Detective Shapiro's phone jangled in his ear unexpectedly. Naturally he spilled his coffee all over the new tie he was wearing. He picked up the phone and heard it was the sherriff of Ely. When he finished he requested that they get together to discuss this situation. They were to meet in Shapiro's office at 9:00 the next morning. The next morning he arrived 5 minutes early for their appointment. He requested a tv with a VCR and showed them the tape. When the tape was done Shapiro looked more confused than ever. He looked again at the tape and then again at the photo of his intake into the jail. It took some doing but he finally realized maybe they put to death the wrong person. He called in Detective Kennedy and John the lead detective in the case. When the story was told again John looked just as confused as Shapiro. He had to explain it for the fifth time. The sherriff asked: "John, did Baxter have a scar on his forehead when you first arrested him?"

John said: "I didn't notice. What are you getting at?"

The sherriff said exasperatedly: "I am trying to say you arrested the wrong man. Do you understand finally?"

John said: "I think so. How do we fix it now though?"

Shapiro said: "We will have to reentries all of the children. Ask them if Baxter had a scar on his forehead. I will start with Jessica. She lives locally and goes to my parish."

John said: "Do you want me to do anything?"

Shapiro said: "Yes John. You can interview Matthew and ask him about the scar. I will give you the address."

29

THE NEXT DAY John set out to seek Matthew's address and do the home visit. When he got there his mother answered the door. She remembered John as being the nice cop who was very gentle with her hysteria. She was most appreciative of this.

John said: "I have to reentries Matthew because of something new that came up.

His mother said: "Of course sir. Please wait here for a minute."

She disappeared upstairs to bring her son down.

John said: "Good morning Matthew. How are you feeling today?"

Matthew said: "I am doing okay. I am seeing a psychiatrist to stop being afraid of the proverbial boogie man. Mom, was it alright to admit to seeing a psychiatrist?"

His mother said: "Of course Matthew. He is a cop and is under strict orders not to gossip about a case or anthing."

John said: "Your mother is right. I don't live here and don't talk to anybody. I also have another secret for you. I talked to a psychiatrist in jail almost every day. I have a prison record, but for minor offenses like carjacking. Don't give up on the psychiatrist. They can be very helpful if you try to give them a chance. Now for the reason I came up here. The man that took you and held you for a year. Did he have a scar on his forehead?"

Matthew thought long and hard about that one and he said that there was a visitor at one point. The two men looked like twins. One had a scar on his forehead, but the other one didn't."

John asked: "Now think really hard. Which one is the one that stayed with you the whole year?"

Matthew said: "The one with the scar is the one that stayed. The one without the scar is the one that left.

I noticed them because they were in the bedroom upstairs together. I was cleaning the gutters and peeked into the bedroom window."

John said: "Thank you Matthew. You have been a big help. By the way. The person who took you has been killed in jail. He was shanked to death in the yard. The other inmates stabbed him. He won't be bothering anybody anymore."

Matthew mother said: "Thank you for telling us. This should make it easier for Matthew to get over this traumatic experience."

John left and reported back to Detective Shapiro. He said Matthew told him that there was a visitor to the house one day. They looked like twins. The one with the scar is the one that held him captive."

Shapiro exploded: "BLOODY HECK !!! DO YOU KNOW WHAT THIS MEANS?"

John said: "Based on your tone of voice I would say it means something bad is about to happen."

Shapiro exploded again: "IT MEANS EINSTEIN THAT WE SENT THE WRONG MAN TO JAIL!!!

THE REAL KIDNAPPER IS STILL OUT THERE!!!

John said "Uh Oh!! I talked to the real kidnapper. Now what do we do?"

Shapiro said: "First we calm down and get ahold of ourselves. We need to think clearly about this. First step is to call the sherriff of Ely and explain to him that we need to arrest this Lucas character. He made the phone call and an all points bulletin was put out for Lucas' arrest."

Detective Shapiro called in Detective John Kennedy for a meeting. He told Kennedy that he wants him to return and reentries Jessica." When he got to Jessica's house he was met by Alice the mother. Alice said: "She is in school right now. Do you have more questions?"

Detective Kennedy said: "Yes mam. Some new evidence has come up. Since Jessica is the one that was there she is the only one that can answer the questions for me. How is she doing by the way?"

Alice said: "She is doing better. She is in second grade now and all caught up with her work. We spend one hour a night reading together."

Detective Kennedy called Detective Shapiro on the

phone right then and there to tell him that she was in school. Shapiro said he will call Sr. Angelus and get her excused from class for a while. But we will do it in the morning."

When he hung up he told Alice what Shapiro had said. Alice had no problem with the detectives talking to Jessica.

30

THE NEXT MORNING Shapiro and Kennedy set out for St. Mark's School. At 9:30 they entered Sr. Angelus' office with a request for a little time with Jessica. Jessica was called to the office and they all sat down in a circle. Sr. Angelus stayed to be the supervisor and witness to the conversation.

Shapiro said: "Good morning Jessica. Do you remember me from last year?"

Jessica said: "Yes I do remember you from the trial that I testified at."

Shapiro said: "Very good Jessica. I have just one question to ask you. The man that you stayed with did he have a scar on his forehead?"

Jessica thought long and hard about it and she said very confidently that he had a scar, but the night before she was rescued another man entered that did not have a scar. The one with the scar left and the one that didn't have the scar stayed with her. They did the old switcheroo."

Shapiro said: " Thank you Jessica. You have been a big help. Go back to class now. I need to talk to Sr. Angelus privately."

Jessica said: "Okay Detective. Bye Sr. Angelus."

Sr. Angelus said: "Bye Jessica. Go straight to class. Don't make any detours."

Jessica said: "Just to the bathroom."

With that she exited the office and off she went.

Sr. Angelus said: "So Detective Shapiro, Kennedy. What is on your mind for today?"

Shapiro said: "Bad news Sr. Angelus. The person we put on trial did not have a scar on his forehead. Jessica just testified that the man who took her had the scar on his forehead."

Sr. Angelus asked: "Are you saying you arrested the wrong man?"

Detective Shapiro said: "I am afraid so Sr. It was Gene the obnoxious lawyer who discovered the mistake. How has Jessica readjusted to not being held captive?"

Sr. Angelus said: "Not very well I'm afraid. She is a very nervous child and she is incontinent. The slightest startling sound and lets her bladder loose. The pediatrician said it was just that she isn't developed in those muscles yet."

Shapiro asked: "Do you believe him?"

Sr. Angelus said: I guess I could see it. I think it is part of the kidnapping scenario though. She is not the only kidnapping victim in this school. I told her she should talk to Paul a 5th grader. He is vey good with talking to little kids.

He is in counseling for the ordeal. PLEASE don't let on that you know this. I was not supposed to let that out."

Shapiro said: "Don't worry. Your secret is safe with me. May I please talk to Paul?"

Sr. Angelus had her secretary paige Paul to the office. When he got there they found he was also very short for his age. Sr. Angelus said to please tell the Detectives how he came about being kidnapped."

Paul went into the story and said that he was a victim of parent kidnapping. He didn't know he was being kidnapped. He thought he was going with his father. His father told him that his mother was sick and he was to go with him for the night. Paul went with him willingly. He stepped out of the motel room to get a snack from the snack machine when a cop asked who he was. He led the cop to the room he was staying at and his father was promptly arrested. He was taken home in a police car back to his mother."

Shapiro said that will be all. He heard enough. They both thanked Sr. Angelus for her time. When they departed they went back to the precinct. He announced Meeting tomorrow morning. The 3 of us will go home for the evening. Get to know our spouses again."

31

THE NEXT MORNING Shapiro came in with a clear head for the meeting. Ovenight he thought about it until his head exploded. He said "The first step is to notify the judge of the error. This is going to give us a black eye, but we can't help what already happened."

Kennedy said: "Judge Michael McClintock is a hard nose for proper behavior. You saw how he interacted with Gene."

Shapiro said: "That was different. He was acting worse than a 4 year old. He got up and said it was his turn. In actuality the judge decides whose turn it is to speak. Then Judge McClintock almost threw him out of the court for being an idiot. You weren't there that day when he told Gene to face the galley and admit to everyone that he was a toad. What is he going to say about our prosecuting the wrong man?"

Kennedy said: "We should call a meeting with Judge McClintock, Elizabeth the prosecutor, and Gene the defense attorney. All we are doing is asking for advice on what we should do next. He can't get mad at that. We are not arguing what questions to ask. He really gets his Irish up when we do that."

The next morning they all adjourned to the judge's chambers and discussed the problem. The judge asked: "Where is this mysterious Lucas now?"

Shapiro said: "He has disappeared, but there is an all points bulletin out for his arrest now. He will be found."

McClintock asked: "How long will it take to find him?"

Shapiro said: "Unfortunately I don't know the answer to that. He claimed to live in that house, but when the sherriff approached him he disappeared into thin air."

McClintock said: "Based on what you said you have enough evidence to start a new trial and put him on the stand. You will also need to put the children back on the stand. They were the only witnesses."

The next day Shapiro hit pay dirt when he got a phone call stating that Lucas has been arrested on unrelated charges. He was to remain in jail until Shapiro and his team come and get him. They left immediately and arrived in Ely at about 4:00 p.m. They battled traffic all the way back home. Lucas was put straight into isolation with no blanket and just a hard bench to lay on. He was stripped on his shoelaces and belt so he can't hang himself. He was check on every 5 minutes. Lucas was proving to be a royal pain in the neck. Most uncooperative prisoner. It was no wonder the sherriff was only too happy to get rid of him. Lucas proved to be loud and cursing a lot. Even the other prisoners wanted to stay away from him. His cursing outdid everyone else. He used swear words they wouldn't dare use in front of their mothers. They wouldn't even use those words to the sherriff when being arrested. Somebody asked the sherriff if the new prisoner had tourret syndrome. The sherriff said he doubted it and believes that he is in full command of his mouth. The sherriff assured the prisoners that he had somebody else coming to take him away. Just hang in there and try not to answer him. When he finally left everyone let out a big sigh of relief. Shapiro had to sign papers releasing the prisoner into his custody. The sherriff's parting words to Shapiro were: "good luck with this one. You will need it. God speed with you."

Shapiro wondered what that meant. 2 blocks into the ride and he figured out what he meant by that. Two hours on the freeway with a potty mouth like that and Shapiro was ready to drive into the river and drown the man. That would mean too much paperwork though.

32

LUCAS WAS ARRAIGNED on Tuesday March 28 in criminal court of Las Vegas, Nevada. He was read the charges against him as kidnapping in the first degree. How do you plead?

Lucas said "Not guilty your honor."

The judge asked: "How are the people on bail?"

The answer came: "The prosecution requests remand without bail your honor. We have new evidence that the wrong man was convicted and sent to jail for this crime."

The judge asked: "Is the wrong man available to testify at this trial?"

The prosecution said: "Unfortunately the wrong man was shanked to death in jail your honor. We do have the children to testify that the man who took them had a scar on his forehead. He went away and came back the night before the children were rescued. The children believe they were twins. One child admitted she thought they did the old switcheroo. As you can see from the defendant he does have a scar on his forehead. The intake pictures of the wrong prisoner show no scar on the forehead."

The judge said: "Remand without bail. Trial will begin in 3 weeks at 9:00 a.m." With that Lucas was carted off to jail. Outside the courtroom Shapiro said 3 weeks is plenty of time to prepare. I will have to notify the parents again of this new trial that they will have to testify for the 2nd time.

33

A WEEK BEFORE THE trial they all interviewed 12 jurors for the case. Nobody tried to get out of it surprisingly. They heard about it on the news when it happened. This was the easiest pick ever of a jury.

Trial began on Monday April 15th at 9:00. Everybody was on time so they began on time. The judge entered the courtroom and the bailiff yelled ALL RISE!!! The honorable Judge McClintock is now in session. The judge said: "Thank you. You may be seated folks." He opened with "I would like all the children to please rise and stand in front of this table on the left." He remembered some of them from the previous trial, except they were a few inches taller and looked smarter. "Now you may sit down. I just wanted to see if I remembered you guys from the last trial. Elizabeth, you may begin with your opening statements please."

Elizabeth said: "Thank you your honor. Ladies and

gentlemen of the jury. During this trial you will hear how a young man lured 5 children into his car and kept them for nearly a year. He was very cunning in how he got them to go with him. He preyed on their vulnerability because they were so young at the time. We thought we had the right man in custody, but after the trial the defense attorney made an unusual discovery. It was the scar on the forehead that gave it away. We already prosecuted the wrong man and convicted him. He was stabbed to death in the jail yard. You must ignore the fact that we got the wrong man. This time we have eyewitness testimony that he is indeed the right man who did this. The first time around nobody thought to ask about the scar."

Gene got up and said "I am the defense attorney. I defended the other guy and told him I would do my best to get him out of jail. I learned of these events, but when I got to the jail to inform him I was informed that he was already dead from being shanked to death in the jail yard. I am only trying to make this right. You must find him guilty on kidnapping."

The judge said: "Elizabeth, call your first witness please."

Elizabeth said: "I call Little Margaret to the stand." As little Margaret approached the stand she was sworn in. Elizabeth asked her : "How old are you now?"

Margaret said: "I am seven years old now."

Elizabeth asked: "Do you remember how and why you were kidnapped?"

Margaret said: "I was playing in the playground with my mother. We were playing hide and seek. She was on one side of the house and I was on the other. Suddenly a man grabbed me from behind and shoved me into a car. I couldn't scream because he was also covering my nose. I couldn't breath either."

Elizabeth asked: "How long were you gone?"

Margaret said: "About a year I guess. When I came home I still couldn't read. I had not opened up a book in the whole time I was kidnapped."

Elizabeth asked: "How did the man treat you when you were there?"

Margaret said: "He hit us a lot. My job was to snap her bra and pull up her zippers and tie her shoes. I couldn't do a lot of that stuff, so he switched me to cleaning the floors."

Elizabeth asked: "Did he hit you?"

Margaret said: "Yes but I kept wetting my pants, so he stopped hitting me. He did beat me for 5 minutes with a cane once. I went into a room that was off limits. I couldn't walk right for 2 days. I had a lot of bruising on my sit upon. The other kids put cream and ointment on me. The cream cleared up the bruising pretty quickly."

Elizabeth asked: "Are you seeing someone about the kidnapping?"

Margaret said: "No. I just picked up my life where I left off. Mom never leaves me alone anyway."

Elizabeth asked: "Are you afraid to leave the house now?"

Margaret said: "Yes. But mom is with me. I am nervous about being in crowds."

Elizabeth asked: "The man that kidnapped you. Is he here in the courtroom today?"

Margaret said: "Yes. There he is over there. He has the scar on his forehead. He had a twin brother that came in and stayed with us. The night before we left he returned and they switched places."

Elizabeth asked: "Where did he go?"

Margaret said: "I don't know. But I didn't think about it until today when I saw him. Nobody asked me about it the first time I testified."

Elizabeth said: "Thank you Margaret. No more questions."

The judge said: "Gene, do you have any questions for this witness?"

Gene said: "Yes your honor. Margaret, when this other person came in was the house dark and dim or was it clearly bright?"

Margaret said: "It was dark and dim. We never had much light. He kept the venetian blinds drawn like a room dimmer. We hardly ever saw any sunshine." \

Gene asked: " How do you know about room dimmers?"

Margaret said: "When I came home mom and I went to buy some venetian blinds. When we looked at the shades we saw the term room dimmers. She explained that is what makes the sun stay out of the room. Little details come back to me when I am not expecting them."

Gene asked: "Now Margaret, you testified that the room was always dim. If that were true how would you have been able to see the scar of figure out if it was there in the first place?"

Margaret said: "I know what I saw and I know what I

remembered. The man that took me had a scar and the man that stayed with me had no scar. Back then nobody asked me about a scar."

Gene said: "Margaret, how do you know he had one if it was dim and dark in the house?"

Margaret said: "Again I say to you. I know what I saw and what happened to me. You weren't there so you shouldn't doubt me."

The judge said: "Enough Gene! She already answered your question. Move on to another one."

Gene said: No more questions your honor."

The judge said: "Thank you Margaret. You may step down.. Elizabeth, call your next witness."

Elizabeth said: "I call Matthew to the stand." As Matthew approached he was sworn in by the bailiff."

As Matthew approached the stand he was sworn in. The bailiff said: "Do you solemnly swear to tell the truth the whole truth and nothing but the truth so help you God?"

Matthew said: "I do."

Elizabeth said: "Matthew, please tell us about the day you were kidnapped."

Matthew said: "I was waiting for the school bus at the corner. Then I was grabbed and shoved into the van. I screamed but nobody heard me. Suddenly everybody came out of nowhere and chased down the van."

Elizabeth asked: "Did he cover your mouth so you couldn't scream?"

Matthew said: "Yes. He also covered my nose. I was in the van before I knew what was happening. He covered me with a blanket. There were no windows in the back of the van."

Elizabeth asked: "How long was this ride in the van?"

Matthew said: "I don't know. It was a long time. I think it was late afternoon when I finally arrived at the house."

Elizabeth asked: "What happened to you when you first got there?"

Matthew said: "He threw me into the chair and laid down the law."

Elizabeth asked: "Did he ever hit you?"

Matthew said: "He hit all of us."

Elizabeth asked: "What did you do in that house?"

Matthew said: "I was to clean the house and help the old lady get dressed. I was supposed to teach Jessica and Margaret how to do zippers and tie laces."

Elizabeth asked: "Were you the oldest child there?"

Matthew said: "I am not sure. We never talked about that."

Elizabeth asked: "Did you use the vacuum cleaner?"

Matthew said: "Yes. But it was too heavy to handle. When I complained about this he beat me with a cane."

Elizabeth asked: "What was the name of the old lady?"

Matthew said: "I don't know. I don't think we ever mentioned it."

Elizabeth asked: "What did you call her hey lady?"

Matthew said: "No. I didn't talk to her much. We were told to work and not speak."

Elizabeth asked: "Did you get a break from no talking?"

Matthew said: "We didn't talk when the man was around. I think the old lady was hard of hearing. We did talk then, but I don't think she realized we were speaking."

Elizabeth asked: "Did you know Margaret and Jessica before the kidnapping?"

Matthew said: "I knew Margaret from school. I didn't know Jessica."

Elizabeth asked: "How many kids were there all together?"

Matthew said: "I think there was 5 of us."

Elizabeth asked: "How did Margaret react to you being there?"

Matthew said: "I think she was relieved to find someone she knew. She seemed to be a bit more relaxed about staying in the house."

Elizabeth asked: "Did the lady hit you or was it always the man?"

Matthew said: "It was always the man. The old lady took swipes at the girls."

Elizabeth asked: "What was Jessica's reaction to being there?"

Matthew said: "She looked like she didn't know what was going on. There was always a look of panic on her face."

Gene jumped up and yelled: "OBJECTION YOUR HONOR"

The judge said; "What is wrong now Gene? Why are you objecting?"

Gene said: "Your honor this child was six years old when

he was taken. How is a six year old going to know about reading people's expressions?"

The judge said: "Overruled!! He has been home for a year now and has learned a lot. You don't know the level of his intelligence. The last statement stays in the record."

Elizabeth asked: "What was different about Jessica than the other kids?"

Matthew said: "Jessica rarely talked. She was a doer, not a talker. We talked at night after everyone was in bed. He thought we were in bed."

Elizabeth asked: "Do you see the person in this courtroom today that took you?"

Matthew said: "Yes. It is the defendant sitting right over there."

Elizabeth said: "We are here today because there was a question about a scar on his forehead."

Matthew said: "The guy that took me had a scar on his forehead. The guy that stayed with me did not have a scar on his forehead."

Elizabeth asked: "What are you doing now to get on with your life?"

Matthew said: "I am seeing a psychiatrist to get over the fear of the proverbial boogie man."

Elizabeth asked: "Is it helping?"

Matthew said: "A little bit. I am nervous being outside."

Elizabeth said: "Thank you Matthew. No more questions your honor."

The judge said: "Gene, do you have any questions for this witness?"

Gene said: "No your honor. But I do reserve the right to recall this witness."

The judge said: "Because of the time we will adjourn until 9:00 tomorrow morning."

34

THE NEXT DAY started at 8:30 in the judge's chambers for a progress report. He wanted the trial over within four days. Both attorneys agreed to finish within four days. He warned Gene about his behavior in court. They were still interviewing children, so he didn't want them confused about what was being asked. He also instructed Gene to stop screaming in court. Gene agreed and promised to behave himself.

At 9:00 all parties entered the courtroom and the bailiff yelled ALL RISE!!! The judge said: "Good morning all. You may be seated."

The judge said: "Elizabeth, call your first witness please."

Elizabeth said: "I call Jessica to the stand."

As Jessica approached the stand she was sworn in. The

bailiff said: "Do you solemnly swear to tell the truth the whole truth and nothing but the truth so help you God?"

Jessica said: "I do."

Elizabeth said: "You may be seated. Now Jessica. Do you remember the day you were taken?"

Jessica said: "Yes. I was in church with my mother praying when somebody took me."

Eizabeth asked: "Do you remember what he said?"

Jessica said: "Yes. He told me Father Raaser had a present for me in the Baptismal Font. I called it the water fountain. I went with him because I would have done anything for Father Raaser. He was the pastor and I liked him. He never talked to me like an idiot. I was a slow child. I never spoke. One thing I liked was going to Mass at 5:00 on Saturday night. I always insisted we go no matter what we were doing. He greeted everybody at the back of the church when they came in."

Elizabeth asked: "Were you ever alone with Father Raaser?"

Jessica said: "No. There was always a female person in the sacristy with me."

Elizabeth asked: "How often did you go to the sacristy with Father Raaser?"

Jessica said: "Not very often. We went there to look at coloring paper. Sr. Angelus had a special word for it."

Elizabeth asked: "I think you mean mimeographed paper."

Jessica said: "Maybe. Your guess is as good as mine."

Elizabeth asked: "Did he ever touch you badly?"

Jessica said: "He wouldn't have done that with Sr.

Angelus there. I remember going to school one day for a visit. Sr. Angelus let me go there for a day and see what kindergarten was all about."

Elizabeth asked: "What were you doing in the church on that Friday?"

Jessica said: "My grandfather had a stroke. We went there to figure out if we should take them off life support."

Elizabeth asked: "Did you understand any of that?"

Jessica said: "No. I just knew we were there. I was to sit there and wait for mom to stop kneeling down and praying."

Elizabeth asked: "What happened when you left the church?"

Jessica said: "I was thrown into the back of the van and driven many hours. There was a window in the ceiling but all I saw was blue sky."

Elizabeth asked: "When did you first realize that you were in trouble?"

Jessica said: "When I got thrown into the van. Father Raaser was not really in there. There was a present in the baptismal font for me. He said Father Raaser was waiting for me outside. He said that Father Raaser knew my name and he was the one that wrote it. I was supposed to meet him outside for a religion lesson."

Elizabeth asked: "Did you go with him willingly?"

Jessica said: "Yes. I never suspected Father Raaser would hurt me or want to harm me. He said he was waiting for me outside, so I went."

Elizabeth asked: "What happened when you finally got to the house?"

Jessica said: " He threw me into a chair and laid down the law. He let me know who was in charge."

Elizabeth asked: "Did he beat you at all?"

Jessica said: "Yes. But I wet myself a lot, so he switched to locking me in the closet."

Elizabeth asked: "Did the old lady ever beat you?"

Jessica said: "No. That was reserved for the man."

Elizabeth asked: "What was the name of the old lady?"

Jessica said: "Gee we never knew. We never called her by name."

Elizabeth asked: "How did she talk to you?"

Jessica said: "She talked very gruffly. Always nasty. She smoked like a chimney."

Elizabeth asked: "Did you have to light a match for her?"

Jessica said: "Fortunately she never asked me to do that. She lit her own cigarette."

Elizabeth asked: "What would have happened to you if you did?"

Jessica said: "I would rather not think about that. Knowing me I probably would have dropped it and set the rug on fire. He really would have been mad then."

Elizabeth asked: "Do you see the person in this courtroom today who took you?"

Jessica said: "Yes. That man right over there took me. He had a scar on his forehead. The man who stayed with me did not have a scar on his forehead."

Elizabeth said: "Thank you Jessica. No more questions your honor."

The judge said: "Gene, do you have any questions for this witness?"

Gene said: "Yes your honor. Now Jessica, are you near sighted?"

Jessica said: "I don't know what that means."

Gene asked: "Look at the last person in the last row. Please stand up."

Jessica said: "I see the person standing very clearly."

Gene said: "Do you see any scars on his face?"

Jessica said: "No. I don't see any scars on his face."

Gene said: "When Elizabeth was questioning you did you notice any scars on her face?"

Jessica said: "No. I didn't notice any scars on her face."

Gene said: "I think you need glasses. As a matter of fact Elizabeth as a chicken pox mark on her face. If you didn't notice that how would you have noticed a scar on the face of the person who took you with a blanket on your face?"

Jessica said: "I am sorry judge. I am not sure what he is saying. What does he mean by all of what he said?"

The judge said: "Don't worry about him Jessica. I understand what he is saying. His job is to caste doubt on what you are saying. I believe you. He is just trying to make you sound unbelievable."

Gene said: "Did you talk to the other children about this trial before you came today?"

Jessica said: "No. I didn't talk to anyone. Mom told me to just answer the questions as best I could. If I didn't know the answer I should tell the judge. If I don't feel comfortable answering I should tell the juge."

Gene asked: "Do you still see Matthew or Margaret?"

Jessica said: "No. They go to a different school than I do.

The judge said: "Because of the hour we will adjourn until tomorrow morning at 9:00. Tomorrow we will interview all the the parents of the children.

35

A T 9:00 THE next morning everybody returned to the courtroom as promised. The bailiff yelled ALL RISE!!! The court in now in session. The judge said: "Good morning everyone. Elizabeth, you may begin when ready.

Elizabeth said: "I call Alice to the stand."

As Alice approached she was sworn in. The bailiff said: "Do you solemnly swear to tell the truth the whole truth and nothing but the truth so help you God?"

Alice said: "I do." She took her seat.

Elizabeth said: "No Alice. Please tell us about the day Jessica disappeared."

Alice said: "We went to church that morning to pray for guidance. My father had a stroke and I had to decide whether or not to take him off life support."

Elizabeth asked: "What was your decision?"

Alice said: "I decided to take him off life support only if

the hospital agreed to donate his organs. They readily agreed and his life came to an end."

Elizabeth asked: "What can you tell us about Jessica's father?"

Alice said; "I would prefer if Jessica was out of the room when I answer that."

The judge said: "Can we get Matthew's mother to remove the 2 children from the courtroom please?"

Matthew's mother got up and took them outside for a little snack in the hall."

The judge said: "All right Alice. Jessica is not here. Please answer the question."

Alice said: "Okay. Jessica was the result of a nice evening gone bad. Somebody slipped me the date rape drug and raped me. I have no memory of the actual rape, but 8 months later here came Jessica. I tell people that Jessica's father was killed in Iraq and that it is just the 2 of us. She doesn't know about my date rape incident. Father Raaser counciled me during that time to have the baby. For some reason I was chosen by God to be this child's mother."

Elizabeth asked: "Did your father know about Jessica's conception?"

Alice said: "Yes. He knew all about date rape. He never made me feel ashamed of what happened."

Elizabeth asked: "Was Jessica a full term baby?"

Alice said: "She was about 2 weeks early. She didn't breath right away when she was born. The lack of oxygen made her slow in development. At the time of her kidnapping she was 4 years old with the development of a 3 year old. She didn't speak too much and then when she did she was not clear at all. I had trouble understanding her. She was a very trying child to raise. I had to hold my temper a lot because I lost patience with her. Father Raaser just told me to keep taking deep breaths and relax.

Elizabeth asked: "When did you first notice Jessica missing?"

Alice said: "About 5 minutes into my prayer time I noticed she wasn't next to me anymore."

Elizabeth asked: "What was your reaction to this discovery?"

Alice said: "I panicked of course. I couldn't figure out why this happened. I ran around the church looking everywhere and calling her name. I was met with total silence."

Elizabeth asked: "Where did you go after this?"

Alice said: "I ran next door to the rectory to find Father Raaser. He answered the door when I rang the bell. He and I both ran back to the church and started searching the church. He instructed me to sit in the last pew and don't move an inch for any reason. I did as I was told. The next thing I knew there was a horse galloping up the aisle. I couldn't believe my eyes. I am still unsure if that was real or if I was hallucinating. Father Raaser looked everywhere. Then I saw the cops coming into the church. The cops moved in to my house for 2 weeks waiting for a ransome note. Nothing ever came. They gave up and decided to take another tactic."

Elizabeth asked: "What did they do?"

Alice said: "You will have to ask them. I do remember the news conference in the church the next day. I was standing there when an old friend of Shapiro's stood up and made a suggestion. I don't remember what that was. I think he made a vague attempt to help somehow."

Elizabeth asked: "What did Father Raaser do?"

Alice said: "He looked in the confessionals and everywhere."

Elizabeth asked: "Was Jessica afraid of the dark?"

Alice said: "Yes. She was terrified of the dark. That is why I figured she was not in the confessional. Father Raaser even checked the boiler. Fortunately the boiler was empty. A lot of things are still fuzzy from that day."

Elizabeth asked: "What did you do when you got home?"

Alice said: "I went through the next year like a zombie. The cops assured me they would not forget about this case. It was 2 weeks and they had nothing."

Elizabeth asked: "When was the next time you heard from Shapiro?"

Alice said: "I think it was almost a year later. He contacted me several times during the year to assure me that they are chasing down leads. Finally he called and said she had been found and he was driving her home. She arrived in a police car with the lights and sirens blaring. She requested that little detail. They obliged."

Elizabeth asked: "What was her physical condition when she returned?"

Alice said: "She was examined by a doctor at a hospital in Ely before I was contacted. She was found to be healthy except for a vitamin deficiency because of a lack of sunlight. They arrived at my house about 1:00 in the morning. The two detectives spent the night in my house because it was too late to send them home. Shapiro went right to sleep as soon as his head hit the couch."

Elizabeth asked: "Do you see the man that took your daughter?"

Alice said: "The first trial took place because everybody was so sure that was the kidnapper. Six months later we discovered there was a twin and now we are doing this all over again."

Elizabeth asked: "Was there a scar on his forehead?"

Alice said: "I do not know of any scar or no scar on his forehead."

Elizabeth said: "Thank you Alice. No more questions your honor."

The judge said: "Gene, do you have any questions for this witness?"

Gene said: "Yes your honor. Now Alice, why were you not paying attention to Jessica?"

Alice said: "What do you mean I wasn't paying attention to her? I was so."

Gene said: "No. According to your testimony you were praying and not looking at her. You know 4 year old children need supervision every minute of the day. If anything it was you that failed to do your job as a parent to look after her."

Elizabeth yelled: OBJECTION!! What does he think he is doing?"

The judge said: "Gene, I warned you. One more time you get out of line and I am holding you in contempt!!"

36

THE JUDGE SAID: "Elizabeth, call your next witness please."

Elizabeth said: "I call Detective Shapiro to the stand."

Detective Shapiro approached the stand and was sworn in. He took his seat.

Elizabeth asked: "Detective Shapiro. Please tell us about St. Patrick's Day of 2010."

Detective Shapiro said: "I was on security detail for the St. Patrick's Day Parade on the strip. I got a call that there was a problem at St. Mark's Church. I am an active parishoner there and am friends with the pastor. I was met at the back doors by Father Raaser the pastor. He took me into the sacristy for a briefing of the situation. He told me that a child is missing from the church. The mother was praying and the child snuck off somewhere unnoticed."

Elizabeth asked: "What did you do when you got the facts?"

Detective Shapiro said: "We stayed in the church to look in the sacristy, the closet, the confessionals, even the boiler. The child was nowhere to be found. I then instructed Detective Kennedy to sit in the back pew with the mother. He talked to her over the next hour. Then we moved into her house for a little waiting game. We were waiting for the phone to ring for a randsome. No call ever came. My newest detective on the team suggested that we hold a news conference in the church to get help from the public. We got a lot of calls from real people and from psychics thinking she was on an Aer Lingus Flight to Ireland. We had to ferret out the crazies from the possible real legitimate claims."

Elizbeth asked: "How did you come about to searching for her?"

Detective Shapiro said: "The next day we went into the school to search the school from top to bottom. The 4 team members and myself, Father Raaser, and Sr. Angelus the principal all were involved in the search. Sr. Angelus, John, and I did the Kindergarten-3rd grade classrooms. We had the most fun with the 1st graders. One asked me where we were when we did the news conference. I told him we were in the church next door. He said: "Oh yeah I thought that background looked familiar." We couldn't help but smile at their innocence. "

Elizabeth asked: "How did John come about to being an acquaintance in your professional life?"

Detective Shapiro said: "Last year I did a case where a ten year old girl was murdered. John made a call to me that he knows information about the case. We went to the jail and interviewed him. He turned his life around when he got out of jail. He tried to use jail to improve his life. When he got out he resettled in Las Vegas and wanted to make a new start. I met him in the supermarket and we talked about him becoming a cop. He excelled in all his classes. Especially the horse training. I was there at his graduation and he started with me. He was the top student. He was there at the news conference and he was in charge of the whole search team. He was the one that found the child."

Elizabeth asked: "What steps did he take to get the child? Did he ride in and sweep her away?"

Detective Shapiro said: "No. He had a certain restraint and protocol to follow. I told him to wait and interview people first. We went to Ely, Nevada and stopped off at the sherriff's office first. We introduced ourselves and explained the situation. We waited until after dark to invade the place. The door was opened by the old lady of the house. John wanted to pull his gun out and pointed it at her, but I had to stop him."

Eizabeth asked: "What was said between John and the old lady?"

Detective Shapiro said: "He asked where was Jessica."

Elizabeth asked: "What was her response?"

Detective Shapiro said: "She screamed that the kids are needed to take care of her. She couldn't take care of herself and they had no money for a nursing home."

Elizabeth asked: "What did John say to that?"

Detective Shapiro said: "He asked who they all were and that they were taking them back home. We found Jessica and they all came out and introduced themselves. They gave us statements in the morning. The first thing we did was to bring them to the local doctor's office for medical exams. Nobody was touched inappropriately. We found no evidence of sexual misconduct on his part."

Elizabeth asked: "Where was Baxter?"

Detective Shapiro said: "He was allegedly working. He came home at 6:00. We were there to meet him and arrest him."

Elizabeth asked: "What happened to the old lady?"

Detective Shapiro said: "The sherriff sent over a social worker to stay with her for the night. Baxter was home the next day and released on his own recognizance. After his arraignment in criminal court he made bail."

Elizabeth asked: "How much was his bail?"

Detective Shapiro said: "I don't remember. By the time he came home all the children were gone."

Elizabeth asked: "What was your first impression of John?"

Detective Shapiro said: "I liked him right away. We were called to the jail in California because he called our hotline and left an anonymous message that he had information on the murder of another child. When we interviewed him he gave us legitimate information. His information led to the arrest of the perpetrator."

Elizabeth asked: "Wasn't he convicted?"

Detective Shapiro said: "No. His execution was all set and we found information that it was his brother who committed these crimes. All he said was that he was willing to go to his death for the sins of his brother. That is what

Jesus Christ did for us. He knew God would not punish him or send him down under for something he did not do."

Elizabeth asked: "How did you come about finding him after John ratted him out?"

Detective Shapiro said: "In my previous case the perpetrator peed his pants and left a puddle on the ground. My Beagle dog sniffed his crotch and came up with a positive ID."

Elizabeth asked: "How did you come about to getting John on your team?"

Detective Shapiro said: "After he got out of jail he wanted to resettle in Las Vegas and start a new life. He turned out to be a model prisoner and the warden and guards made his life easy. As long as he never screwed up he was on their good side. The guards said it was just a temporary stop and that it was possible to do his time and get on with his life. That is what he chose to do."

Elizabeth said: "Thank you Detective Shapiro. No more questions your honor."

The judge said: "Gene, do you have any questions for this witness?"

Gene asked: "When did you arrest my client?"

Detective Shapiro said: "About a month ago.

Gene asked: "Wasn't Baxter's case closed after he was put in jail?

Detective Shapiro said: "Yes, but you were the one who said he was innocent. You were the one who first noticed the scar on his forehead."

Gene said: "Isn't it true that you prosecuted the wrong man for this crime?"

Detective Shapiro said: "Yes. We did prosecute the wrong man. He was sent to jail and he was shanked to death in the yard."

Gene asked: Doesn't this make you responsible for the death of an innocent man?"

The judge said: "Watch it Gene. You are supposed to defend the defendant and not prosecute the arresting officer."

Gene said: "Sorry your honor. There is a law on the books that states somebody is responsible for a death if it was false allegations."

Detective Shapiro said: "I am familiar with this law you are referring to. This one does not apply here because it wasn't me who made these allegations. He was innocent, but it was your job to prove that and you are a failure at it. Since he was found guilty you were supposed to convince everyone we were wrong. You didn't do that, so don't put that on me."

The judge said: "Gene, move on. Do you have any real questions for this witness?"

Gene said: "No your honor."

The judge said: "We will adjourn for the day. Gene, meet me in my office at 8:30 tomorrow morning."

Gene and Elizabeth both said yes sir simultaneously.

37

A T 8:30 THE next morning Elizabeth and Gene both reported to the judge's chambers. The judge was mortified that Gene would have the nerve to blame Detective Shapiro for the screw ups of himself. He reminded Gene that he needs to go back to school and take a refresher course on the law and what applies to what situations. He reminded Gene that if it wasn't for his ineptness the jury would have found him not guilty. They returned to the courtroom and 9:00. The bailiff yelled: "ALL RISE!!!" The judge said: "Good morning everyone. You may be seated. Elizabeth, call your first witness please."

Elizabeth said: "I call John to the stand." As John approached the stand he was sworn in by the bailiff. Do you solemnly swear to tell the truth the whole truth and nothing but the truth so help you God?"

John said: "I do."

The bailiff said: "You may be seated."

Elizabeth said: "John, please tell the court how you got to know Detective Shapiro."

John said: "I believe Detective Shapiro already answered that question/"

Elizabeth said: "Yes, but we need to hear it from your own words."

John said: "All right. Last year I was in jail for carjacking. My cell mate kept broadcasting that he murdered a ten year old girl. He got out early because the arresting officer forgot to read him his Miranda rights. After he left I contacted Shapiro because he had to pay for his crimes. In the jail world killing or harming a child or raping a woman is the lowest of the low. He had to pay for his crime. I didn't know about him taking the rap for his brother until I read it in the papers.

Elizabeth asked: "Let's back up a bit. How did you first meet Detective Shapiro?"

John said: "When I got out of jail I came to Las Vegas to live because I wanted a fresh start. I got a job at the Motel 6 on the strip across from the Mandalay Bay. The manager encouraged me to start going to church. Then he got me an apartment. When I was doing one of my first shopping trips I ran into Detective Shapiro down the bread isle. He encouraged me to become a cop. He guided me through the whole process. I ended up excelling in all aspects of police training. My boss at the Motel 6 encouraged me all along. I couldn't wait to get there on Saturday and share my week with him. For some reason I was chosen to do mounted police training for a while. The first time I mounted a horse

I ended up facing the tail end of it. It took everybody 20 minutes to stop laughing. I couldn't believe I did something like that. The sergeant said not to worry. Everybody is entitled to one screw up every now and then."

Elizabeth asked: "Was there really a horse in the church?"

John said: "Yes. When we heard there was a problem in the church the horse took off like a rocket. I couldn't get him to stop until we reached the altar rail."

Elizabeth asked: "What was Shapiro's reaction to this?"

John said: "He almost had a proverbial stroke. The pastor got a good tickle out of it. He couldn't help but laugh and make goo goo noises with the horse. Shapiro kept saying FOCUS PLEASE."

Elizabeth asked: "What were you told to do at the church?"

John said: "I was told to sit in the back pew with the mother and calm her down. I was told to just hold her hand and make sure she doesn't run away or anything."

Elizabeth asked: "What was your next move?"

John said: "My next move was to escort her down to the police station. We questioned her yet again about her activities and how the child came about to disappear. We fed her a hot meal and a hot cup of coffee. She ate, but barely tasted it."

Elizabeth asked: "What did you feed her?"

John said: "I don't remember that detail. It seemed unimportant."

Elizabeth asked: "What did you do the next day?"

John said: "The next day we did the news conference at the church. Then the day after that we did the Code Adam at the school. We searched the school from top to bottom. No tile was left unturned. We split up into 3 teams and were escorted by Sr. Agnelus and Father Raaser. Each one of them took one group. Then we did the boiler room and the basement and the rooftop. Meantime we had helicopters flying overhead looking at things that might suggest a problem. I was in the group that did the K-3 classrooms. The 1st graders were the most fun. They had questions and were not afraid to ask. Some of the 3rd graders wanted to see my gun. Then some wanted to see my badge. One recognized the church as the background, but couldn't place where he saw it before. Hey he was only a 1st grader. Sr. Angelus supervised us the whole time. We finished by the end of the day. It didn't take too long. We canceled the Code Adam."

Elizabeth asked: "What happened after you went public with this news conference?"

John said: "After the news conference we had to ferret out the possible sightings from the obvious not ones. Shapiro put me in charge of the searches. We decided to search the Motel 6, the play area of Burger King, and then move on to the Liberace Museum. First we did one building and then the other building. We met with no resistance at all because we announced a Code Adam. Everybody knew what it meant. We dealt with a lot of tourists, so we had to go back and explain everything as to who we were looking for.

The second building Shapiro got distracted and wanted to know the explanation of all of the exhibits including the

Monstrance and all of his costumes. I did the first building where there were a lot of cars. I searched the trunks and back seats of all of the cars and even heard an explanation of their history. I think I saw his first typewriter. I had to wear gloves to prevent my bodily oils from seeping into his cars. That means I wasn't allowed to physically touch any display. It was funny that the tour guide didn't know anything about the monstrance because she was Jewish. She didn't know the proper terms of the items. She came up with the story that his cousin was a priest, so he came to the house every Sunday and celebrated Mass at 2:00 in the afternoon. Liberace didn't want to go to Mass because he was afraid he would be a distraction from the Mass. People would watch him and not the priest. I learned a lot about the man on that visit."

Elizabeth said: "Please tell us about searching the hotel rooms."

John said: "Shapiro told me I was in charge of this operation. I told him we had to search the hotel rooms. He almost fell off the chair. He said: "Please tell me he didn't just say that." He thought I was a nut. He said it would be impossible. I proved him wrong. We started in the New York New York and we called a Code Adam. The managers immediately went to lock all the exits and security was posted to explain the problem."

Elizabeth asked: "Did you go to New York New York hotel?"

John said: "No. I started in the Flamingo across the street. I had Detective Joseph Kennedy with me. We adjourned at the end of the day for a meeting first thing in the morning in Shapiro's office. We even stopped the cops along the strip as we went along."

Elizabeth asked: "Did you have a picture of Jessica with you?"

John said: "Detective Joseph Kennedy had some. All of the stores gladly put up a picture in their window."

Elizabeth asked: "How long did this search take of the hotel rooms?"

John said: "The first two didn't take too long. We were pretty organized. We even searched the rooftops of the hotels."

Elizabeth said: "Let's switch gears for a moment. Let's move on to you finding Jessica."

John said: "I traced a call from a supposed psychic. Shapiro told me I was wasting my time, but I insisted on going to check it out anyway. When I got there the woman was very unfriendly. She said it was about time I got there. She showed me a video tape that she got a hold of. She was visiting a friend of hers and she saw the kids outside. She knew they were missing kids because she saw their profile on a TV show that does this. They pick kids out and do their story. Then we saw Jessica still wearing the pink polka dotted dress and sandals she was wearing the day she disappeared."

Elizabeth asked: "What did you do at that point?"

John said: I wanted to run in and rescue the kids, but we had protocol to worry about. I almost ran into Shapiro when I ran him down to tell him. I had the video tape and showed it to Shapiro. He almost swallowed his sandwich whole. We made a plan to go into Ely, Nevada the next day and get the child. Then we found there were 5 missing children."

Elizabeth asked: "Did you contact the sherriff first or did you run in?"

John said: "When we got to Ely we went straight to the sherriff and explained who we were. We showed him the video tape and he knew exactly where the house was and who lived in it."

Elizabeth asked: "Did she give up the kids right away?"

John said: "No. We had to coax her to give them up. One of them came out to see who was at the door. I asked Matthew for Jessica and he went to get her. Then he got 3 other kids as well. When we got them Baxter drove up unexpectedly and went totally postal. He started screaming and cursing at everybody who was within ear shot. His mother was assigned to an adult social worker while Baxter was being questioned."

Elizabeth asked: "What was the condition of the house?"

John said: "The house was immaculate. The kids were brought down to the police station to be interviewed one at a time. The sherriff suggested we take them to the town doctor. We did that and then we drove them home. We informed the parents that the interviews were finished but we needed them to testify in court anyway. Surprisingly the all agreed. The children were found to be healthy except for a vitamin deficiency because of a lack of sunlight."

Elizabeth said: "Lets get back to the horse for a minute.

I just can't let that one go. What did you do with the horse and why were you in possession of it?"

John always smiled when he spoke about the horse. He said: "Actually when I did my training as a cop because I excelled in all my classes I was specially chosen to do mounted assignments. I had to dress the horse, clean its stall, and give him water and food every night. At night when we finished our shift I had to undress the horse, clean its stall, and give him water and food for the night. I must have good charma because the horse took to me right away. The seargeant said I was very lucky when it came to that. Most horses take time and put up a fuss about being ridden. I had to wash the horse also. "

Elizabeth said: "Please explain the term dress the horse."

John said: "That means that I put on its saddle, its bridle, and checked his overall body for troubled spots. I had to observe the behavior and wait for the horse to tell me something. He only whinnied at me when I came in. He knew me right away. He knew right away what was coming."

Elizabeth asked: "Did you get special training to figure out what was wrong with the horse?"

John said: "Of course. I come from California and we never lived with horses or anything like that. I never even looked at a horse until I came to this class."

Elizabeth asked: "Was there a reward for leading the cops to an arrest and conviction of the killer of this Sarah?"

John said: "I don't think so. If there was I never received it. I never did it for money. I did it to get justice for this little girl. She never deserved to have that happen. Let me just say one thing about that. He was arrested and convicted, but it turned out to be the wrong person. The cops had to do an investigation first to check their facts."

Elizabeth said: "No more questions your honor."

The judge said: "Gene, do you have any questions for this witness?"

Gene said: "Yes your honor. Now John, how did the cops catch this person?"

John said: "Apparently the perpetrator peed his pants and left a puddle under him. The puddle was not under the person hanging. One of his partners was given the task of getting the urine up from the ground and preserving it for DNA. The lab came up with the DNA profile. The Beagle dog sniffed the crotch of the perpetrator and sat down. That was the signal that there was a match."

Gene said: "Your honor I move to strike this whole testimony. First the cops use a Beagle dog the arrest the perpetrator and then they use a cat in another case that was sighted last week in the Salt Lake City Utah newspaper. The cat scratched the burglar and they got the burglar's blood stains from the mouth of the cat. Next week I will bet they will use a goldfish to catch the next perpetrator."

At this point Shapiro jumped up and screamed IDIOT YOU WERE THE ONE WHO BROUGHT THIS CASE TO OUR ATTENTION!!!"

The judge said: "SHAPIRO SIT DOWN AND SHUT UP OR LEAVE THE COURTROOM!!!"

Detective Shapiro said: "My apologies your honor. I was

wrong and I know that was uncalled for. He just gets me fired up sometimes."

The judge said: "That's all right Shapiro. Gene, keep a lid on it and get back into the game.

We will adjourn for the day and just meet me in my office tomorrow morning at 8:30."

38

A T THE MORNING meeting in the judge's chambers there was a lot of warnings going out about not screaming out in court. He asked: "How much longer is this trial going to take?"

Elizabeth said: "Not much longer your honor., We should be finished by the end of the week."

The judge said: "See to it. I want no excuses for not finishing."

Both Elizabeth and Gene agreed to behave themselves. They returned to the courtroom by 9:00 and they resumed the case. Elizabeth, call your next witness please.

Elizabeth said: "I call Detective John Kennedy to the stand." As Detective John Kennedy approached the stand he was sworn in by the bailiff. He said: "Do you solemnly swear to tell the truth the whole truth and nothing but the truth so help you God?"

Detective Kennedy said: "I do." He took his seat and waited for Elizabeth to begin.

Elizabeth said: "Detective Kennedy, how long have you worked with Detective Shapiro?"

Detective Kennedy said: "I have known him and worked with him for maybe 3 years now."

Elizabeth asked: "Do you believe you know Detective Shapiro well?"

Detective Kennedy said: "Yes. We have a good repoire together. We take turns renting cars and doing interviews."

Elizabeth asked: "Whose idea was it to search the school from top to bottom?"

Detective Kennedy said: "That was Ronald's idea. Ronald was the father of the child who was murdered last year."

Elizabeth asked: "When did he come up with this idea and why was he sticking his nose into the police business?"

Detective Kennedy said: "He suggested it at the news conference and he wasn't really sticking his nose into our business. He had his daughter with him. She was asleep in the carriage. Ronald is the former altar boy partner of Detective Shapiro. After Sarah's death they kept in touch with each other. They remained friends."

Elizabeth asked: "Does Detective Shapiro entertain Ronald a lot?"

Detective Kennedy said: "You will have to ask him that. He was only trying to help. They remained mutual and respectable friends. "

Elizabeth asked: "Does he entertain you at all?"

Detective Kennedy said: "No. Our relationship is only professional. We never talked about getting together on a social level."

Elizabeth asked: "Whose team were you on during the search of the school?"

Detective Kennedy said: "I was on John's team with Detective Shapiro. My job was to go to his house and pick him up at 6:00 a.m. John and I arrived and his wife let us in. He is notoriously late for every appointment he makes. We wanted to be punctual. He is a very deep sleeper, so we had to pull of the blankets and practicall tip the mattress upside down. Finally he moved. We started to question whether or not he was dead. He trudged into the shower and came out 15 minutes later looking better. He said it was a cold shower and it was the only thing that woke him up. His dog even tried to lick his face. He pawed at him. John considered calling EMS, but finally he moved. I had to restrain him from doing so. We got to the diner and ate a heavy meal and drank a lot of coffee. Then we had to get rid of it. That took an extra half hour because there was only one toilet in there. We got to the school and Sr. Angelus almost fell over with surprise because we were on time. We explained that we brought him to breakfast and that is the only reason he is on time. We were all set to get started when we all had to use the bathroom again. We used the student's bathroom because there were 10 urinals in there. The teacher's lounge only had one toilet. To save time all 6 of us went at the same time."

Gene asked: "How long did this search take?"

Detective Kennedy said: "I think we were finished by 11:00. We were split up into 3 groups."

Gene asked: "Were you involved in the search of the Liberace Museum?"

Detective Kennedy said: "Yes. I was in the other building from John when I did that. Detective Shapiro was more interested in the exhibits than why we were really there. I had to reign him in and refocus his attention. I looked at it as a gift. I got to see a museum for free. That doesn't happen too often."

Gene asked: "What about the search of the hotel rooms on the strip?"

Detective Kennedy said: "I was not on John's team for that. I was one of the people who searched the Bellagio hotel. In the mean time John and Detective Shapiro was in the Flamingo across the street."

Gene said: "Lets' get back to Ronald for a minute. You said Ronald had a daughter with him in a carriage?"

Detective Kennedy said: "Yes. He did."

Gene asked: "Is this his birth daughter?"

Elizabeth said: OBJECTION YOUR HONOR!! What does this have to do with finding the missing child?"

The judge said: "You are right Elizabeth. Just let him hang himself with these irrelevant questions. I will instruct the jury to disregard. You may answer the question Detective Kennedy."

Detective Kennedy said: "That is not his birth daughter. About six months after the perpetrator was put to death Shapiro got a visit from a teenager carrying a baby. She asked about the baby safe haven law. She wanted to put her up for adoption, but was afraid of being arrested for child abandonment. Detective Shapiro promised her that wasn't going to happen. He offered her a ride home in a police car. He also offered her a telephone to let her parents know she is coming home. I drove her home myself. Her parents thank me profusely for looking after her. I did meet her a year later and we were told she graduated with honors from high school. She was on her way to college. We were all elated to hear she was getting her life back together. She did not ask about the baby. Shapiro decided to give the baby to Ronald and Eloise since their daughter was murdered. He was in fine form when he brought the baby in. Ronald didn't even think twice about taking her in."

Gene asked: "Did the baby get adopted legally?"

Detective Kennedy said: "I don't know. We never talked about it."

Elizabeth jumped up and asked what that has to do with the case?"

Gene said: "I am talking about her because I am wondering why friends of cops get special privileges. Any ordinary person would get a visit from a social worker. What else has Detective Shapiro done? Who else does he bend the rules for?"

Detective Kennedy said: "That's enough. We all love and respect each other professionally and personally. I supported Detective Shapiro in anything he wanted to do with the baby. We all thought it was a bright idea to give her to Ronald. For your information Gene we saw Ronald through diabetes complications and worries. They were the best parents we ever met."

Gene asked: "If they are so perfect parents why did they let Sarah go off by herself so early in the morning?"

Detective Kennedy said: "Judge, there are facts about this case that Gene doesn't know about. Why is he bringing this up?"

The judge said: "Detective Kennedy, what information is Gene missing?"

Detective Kennedy said: "We found out after the funeral that Sarah was huffing and that is why she was getting into trouble all the time. Everybody knew something was wrong, but nobody ever figured it out."

Gene asked: "How did the people around her react to her huffing?"

Detective Kennedy said: "They all knew something was wrong, but Detective Shapiro was one person she seemed to have listened to. He was called in to the school to diffuse several situations."

The judge said: "The jury is instructed to ignore this whole testimony. Sarah's case has no bearing on this one. Gene, get back on subject."

Gene said: "No more questions your honor."

The judge said: "You may step down Detective Kennedy. Elizabeth, call your next witness."

Elizabeth said: "I call Mary Kelly to the stand."

As Mary approached the stand the bailiff swore her in. He said: "Do you solemnly swear to tell the truth the whole truth and nothing but the truth so help you God?

Mary said: "I do. She took a seat.

Elizabeth asked: "What is your occupation?"

Mary said: "I am the warden of the jail in California."

Elizabeth asked: "Was John ever in your jail?

Mary said: "Yes he was. I do remember him as a prisoner in my jail."

Elizabeth asked: "What kind of prisoner was he?"

Mary said: "When he first arrived he was an angry and very upset person. I put 4 of my best guards on him and they worked with him. They helped him adjust to jail life. He also saw the psychiatrist two times a week. He calmed down after that. He started to feel better and really look at us, but look through us."

Elizabeth asked: "Did he have to endure the strip searches?"

Mary said: "Yes. Everybody endures those. They are just a part of life in jail."

Elizabeth asked: "Did he have to endure the drug testing?"

Mary said: "Yes. He had to endure those too."

Elizabeth asked: "Did he ever refuse the drug tests and strip searches?"

Mary said: "No. He never refused. He wanted to cooperate and then he became a model prisoner. Our guards guided him in the direction of being a model prisoner. He never gave us any trouble."

Elizabeth asked: "When did he take in interest in his former cellmate?"

Mary said: "The guards allowed him a phone call to a Detective Shapiro. He explained that the murder of Sarah was done by his former cellmate. He had information that was not released to the press."

Elizabeth asked: "What was your reaction to his knowing this?"

Mary said: "I told him if his conscience told him to say something then he should do it. I stepped back and let him do all the talking. When Detective Shapiro came to the jail we just sat there and listened to whatever he had to say. The guards didn't interrupt him either. They were really trying to remember what part of what he was saying even sounded plausible."

Elizabeth asked: "Was there a reward for him coming forward with information?"

Mary said: "Not to my knowledge. Nobody ever talked about him getting anything."

Elizabeth asked: "Do you keep in touch with John?"

Mary said: "I had a few phone calls from Detective Shapiro. He gave me an update that John is now a cop. He told me he excelled in all of his classes especially horse training."

Elizabeth asked: "Did this surprise you when you heard that?"

Mary said: "No. I always knew he could do anything he put his mind to. He always had the potential to learn. When he got into the cop academy he surprised himself. He had a reason to get up in the morning. "

Elizabeth asked: "How did he get to Las Vegas from California?"

Mary said: "Our guards drove him. It took 8 hours one way. The guards took an extra day off for that assignment. They did not hang out with him or anything like that. They just dropped him off at the Motel 6 and wished him well."

Elizabeth asked: "Do you have any contact with John now?"

Mary said: "No. He has never contacted me for anything."

Elizabeth asked: "What do you do to reform prisoners?"

Mary said: "Two of our guards are former drill sergeants. They use that part of their lives to reform prisoners. We have had no returns of prisoners since the program started. They have to pass a rigorous admission program. They can't be known for spitting or throwing bodily fluids on the guards. They have to be nonviolent offenders."

Elizabeth asked: "Did Baxter ever take these classes?"

Mary said: "Yes, but he flunked out. He refused to play the game by the rules. He was put in the corner and he had to do multiple situps and pushups. Nothing worked. He didn't even like the haircut. They guards had to practically strap him down to get the haircut."

Elizabeth asked: "How did he come about getting stabbed?"

Mary said: "He was shanked to death in the yard. Even though we do strip searches sometimes they still manage to get weapons through. They are a lot smarter than we think they are.

Elizabeth asked: "Did you ever catch the guy that did it?"

Mary said: "Yes. We gave him 30 days in the hole and an extra year tagged on to his sentence. He was actually there for life, but we had to send a message that this kind of thing will not be tolerated."

Elizabeth said: "Thank you Mary. No more questions your honor.

The judge said: "Gene, do you have any questions for this witness?"

Gene said: "Yes your honor. Now Mary, why did you allow Baxter to be stabbed?"

Mary said: "I believe we already established that. I did not allow it, but sometimes it just happens without being in our control."

Gene said: "I believe you are responsible for the death of Baxter because it happened on your watch and it was your negligence that brought the events into being."

The judge said: "That's enough Gene. The person on trial here is Lester, not Baxter."

39

THE NEXT DAY started at 8:30 in the office of the judge's chambers. The judge asked: "Gene, how many witnesses do you have?"

Gene said: "Just a few sir. It won't take long. I promise."

The judge said: "See to it Gene. I have other cases to deal with and you have 2 days to finish."

Gene said: "Yes sir. I understand."

At 9:00 everybody adjourned to the courtroom to start the day. The judge said: "Good morning folks."

Everybody responded "Good morning judge."

The judge said: Elizabeth, do you have anymore witnesses?"

Elizabeth said: "No sir. The prosecution rests."

The judge said: "Very well. Gene, call your first witness please."

Gene said: "I call Lester to the stand." As Lester approached the stand he was sworn in. The bailiff said: "Do you solemnly swear to tell the truth the whole truth and nothing but the truth so help you God?"

Lester said: "I do." He took his seat.

Gene said: "Lester, please tell us who you are."

Lester said: "My name is Lester Jones. I am the one who took the children."

Gene asked: "Where did you grow up?"

Lester said: "I grew up in the city of Perth, Oregon."

Gene asked: "When did you move to Ely, Nevada?"

Lester said: "We moved here after my mother had her stroke. We couldn't afford a nursing home, so we had to take care of her ourselves."

Gene asked: "Who is Baxter to you and how is he related to you?"

Lester said: "Baxter was my adopted brother. He wasn't even related to us by blood. He was adopted as a child. He was not related to any of us. He stayed with us as times got hard."

Gene asked: "Did he know he was adopted?"

Lester said: "Yes. He knew all along."

Gene asked: "Did he remember his birth parents?"

Lester said: "No. He never remembered them or talked about them or even asked about them. He was adopted as a baby."

Gene asked: "Who took the children?"

Lester said: "I took the children, but Baxter stayed with them the whole time. I took off for a year. I came home only when my brother needed another kid."

Gene asked: "Where were you when you took off?"

Lester said: "I was on a skiing holiday and got a job there. I was in the Swiss Alps. They have snow all year long there."

Gene asked: "Did your mother know which son was in the house with her?"

Lester said: "If she did she never let on to it. She never called us by name. When I showed up she was in her room. I don't know if she was aware of my presence."

Gene asked: "How did you pay for the house that you lived in?"

Lester said: "We won it in a lawsuit. We got paid the whole thing at once."

Gene asked: "How much was this lawsuit worth?"

Lester said: "We got $50,000.00 at once."

Gene asked: "Who did you sue?"

Lester said: "We sewed the hospital emergency room because she laid on the gurney for 16 hours and didn't get seen. We went in an ambulance and they still wouldn't see us. By the time she got her MRI the blood vessels started to heal themselves."

Gene asked: "How long did it take for your mother to start walking again?"

Lester said: "It took maybe a year. She had to work on her own. She finally walked with a cane."

Gene asked: "Did she have in home physical therapy?"

Lester said: "Yes. But that lasted only until the money ran out. Then we got the lawsuit settled. That is when we moved to Ely, Nevada."

Gene asked: "What made you pick Ely, Nevada to move to?"

Lester said: "We saw it profiled on TV. It was a small town and we liked the looks of it. Friendly people. The episode we saw was a dog that got lost and came home after a month of wandering the mountains. My mother liked the mountains because that is where we always grew up. "

Gene asked: "Were you happy in Ely, Nevada?"

Lester said: "I hadn't spent enough time there to judge it."

Gene asked: "How did Baxter feel about it?"

Lester said: "Baxter always had the personality of a person who didn't talk much. He had no expression on his face and a blank look in his eyes. He was always that way."

Gene asked: "Why was he like that?"

Lester said: "He was probably born that way. He never talked about his life before we met him. As he got older that blank look was more prominent."

Gene asked: "When did you first hear of your mother's death?"

Lester said: "I first heard it when I got home and found nobody there. Then I met you and you told me everything that happened."

Gene asked: "How did you get that scar on your forehead?"

Lester said: "I got it from a fall in a playground as a kid. I fell on some glass. Me and Baxter always fooled around and got rough with each other."

Gene asked: "Do you remember the circumstances of your cut on your head?"

Lester said: "All I remember is swinging on the swings and then falling off. Baxter started chasing me and then I lost my balance. That is when I fell to the ground. I remember all the blood. Apparently head injuries bleed like a banshee. My mother beat the crap out of us the next week for getting too rough with each other. Baxter couldn't walk for a week. I couldn't sit down for a week either."

Gene asked: "What did she beat you with?"

Lester said: "Anything she could find. I think it was a paddle or something. Like wha the fraternities have. Only she wailed on me for endless minutes. It might have been 3 minutes or 5 minutes. After the first 10 wacks you go numb and don't feel anything anymore. I still have no feeling on my sit upon. I don't know if my rear end is touching the chair or not."

Gene asked: "Have you had this checked out with a doctor?"

Lester said: "No. What would be the point? I have lived with it all my life. There is probably nerve damage in there. Why open up old wounds? I refuse to go through the humiliation of exposing my bottom for some stranger to go around poking up there."

Gene asked: "Did Baxter have the same injuries you did?"

Lester said: "We never talked about it. Why humiliate myself by admitting I was injured. I was supposed to be the man and take it like one."

Gene asked: "Where was your father in all of this?"

Lester said: "He was always working. When mom told him what happened he praised her for it. He said it would toughen me up. He said to teach me not to cry or scream. When he came in he wailed on me again. This one was with the strap. I didn't feel any of it. When Baxter looked at my bottom he saw I was completely black and blue. He couldn't believe it. All he said was he was glad it wasn't him. An hour later our father heard this and came in and strapped him with his belt all over again."

Gene asked: "What was ever done about it?"

Lester said: "About a month later Baxter worked up the nerve to ask why he did that all the time. Our father explained that when you are a man you need to give punishment to your own children, so you need to learn to take it."

Gene asked: "Was Baxter punished for asking about this?"

Lester said: "Our father punched his fist on the table and said to go to bed. He was in charge and that was all there was to it. We didn't realize that he could sit in the living room and listen to our conversations by the fireplace. That is how he got all our secrets. He died of a sudden cardiac arrest one Spring day on the job. That was the end of him and we never talked about him again."

Gene asked: "How did your mother respond to your father's death?"

Lester said: "Our mother didn't respond at all. She just carried on as if he never existed. He was gone so much and for so long that she was used to being on her own."

Gene asked: " What about your grandparents?"

Lester said: "They were just as abusive as our parents were. They thought nothing of beating the crap out of us for the slightest little infarction."

Gene asked: "Were you beaten by them also?"

Lester said: "Yes. The slightest little thing set them off. We couldn't complain because our mother would beat us for making them angry. They were old and needed to relax. We were there to help them, not aggravate them. Usually she would hit us on out back or legs, which was a relief from being hit on the bottom. She also used her cane to wail on us."

Gene asked: "In your opinion did Baxter do this because this is what he was taught?"

Lester said: "Everybody knows that's how the story goes. You get beat so you beat someone else."

Gene said: "Thank you Lester. No more questions your honor."

The judge said: "Elizabeth, do you have any questions for this witness?"

Elizabeth said: "Yes your honor. Now Lester, you say you were beaten all the time by your mother. Why didn't you run away?"

Lester said: "Baxter did that once and he was beaten physically with the strap. The cops brought him home when he was found to be out too late after dark. They thought they were doing a good thing by saving his life."

Elizabeth asked: "Did you ever fight back with your parents?"

Lester said: "No. I never fought back. I just wanted it to stop as soon as possible."

Elizabeth asked: "When did you first realize that this was wrong?"

Lester said: "I guess when I was maybe thirteen and I

became a teenager. Then mom threatened me with military school, so I slapped her face as hard as I could. Oddly enough she never laid a hand on me again. That was the end of the abuse. She must have saw something in my face that said touch me and I will kill you. I forgave her when she was on her death bed with the stroke."

Elizabeth asked: "Where are you living now?"

Lester said: " I am living in the jail until the trial is over. When I am found not guilty I don't know where I will live."

Elizabeth said: "IF you are found not guilty."

Lester said: "That's right. But I am confident of the legal system. All I did was snatch the kids. Baxter was the one who abused them and beat them black and blue. I just showed up after a year's absence."

Elizabeth said: "No more questions your honor."

The judge said: "Gene, call your next witness please."

Gene said: "I call Martin Smith to the stand."

As Martin approached the stand he was sworn in by the bailiff. He said: "Do you solemnly swear to tell the truth the whole truth and nothing but the truth so help you God?"

Martin said: "I do." He took his seat.

Gene said: "Now Martin, please tell us your occupation and how you are related to this case."

Martin said: "I am a guard at the jail. I was assigned to protect Baxter from being shanked or attacked at the jail."

Gene asked: "Why did you fail in your duties to protect him?"

Martin said: "I turned my head to look at a disturbance down in the pit. That is when they got Baxter. I was talking on the walkie talkie and then I heard the commotion behind me. He was a most wanted man in the jail world. His crimes were unspeakable."

Gene asked: "How did Baxter die?"

Martin said: "He was stabbed in the ribs, but to complicate the matter he was stabbed in such a way that his lung collapsed. It was a classic military move that you learn in basic training. You can kill a person without the bloodshed. You don't get your clothes or hands dirty that way."

Gene asked: "This person that did this. Was he in the military?"

Martin said: "I don't know. I don't know the history of every prisoner."

Gene asked: "Did Baxter take the classes for boot camp training?"

Martin said: "Yes he did. But he flunked out. Even the other prisoners didn't want to be around him. He was dismissed back to the general population."

Gene asked: "Is this when he was stabbed?"

Martin said: "Yes. About a month after his return."

Gene asked: "How long was Baxter's visits to the yard?"

Martin said: "He got an hour in the yard every day. Then he was returned to his cell."

Gene asked: "Did Baxter ever fail the drug tests?"

Martin said: "No. He never failed."

Gene asked: "Why did Baxter take the heat for his brother?"

Martin said: "You will have to ask him for that. He never talked about it."

Gene said: "No more questions your honor."

The judge said: "Elizabeth, do you have any questions for this witness?"

Elizabeth said: "Yes your honor I do. Now Martin, when did you first discover that Baxter had been stabbed in the ribs?"

Martin said: "Right after it happened. When I turned around to look I saw him on the ground and blood was seeping into his shirt. That is when I called for a gurney to come to the yard."

Elizabeth asked: "Why didn't you call an ambulance right away?"

Martin said: "Because it happened on jail property. We try to take care of our own prisoners whenever possible. We are equipped to do minor surgeries like tatoo removal and appendectomies and tonsilectomies, but major surgeries like gall bladder removal and liver removal is sent out to the hospital for."

Elizabeth asked: "How did you know it wasn't his gall bladder?"

Martin said: "Because if your gall bladder stops functioning you don't have blood all over your shirt. Besides the gall bladder is on the right side. His blood was on the left side and seeping through. It was more above where the gall bladder is."

Elizabeth asked: "At what point did you call the ambulance?"

Martin said: "When we got him into the infirmary and cut off his shirt that is when we called the ambulance."

Elizabeth asked: "How long did it take to get him to the hospital?"

Martin said: "The ambulance was called and they arrived within 3 minutes. The guards at the gate were called and were waiting for them. They escorted the group into the infirmary. Then he was taken to the hospital. It was a timing of maybe 5 minutes. The paramedics had to assess what the problem was and then call ahead to the hospital."

Elizabeth asked: "Didn't the house doctor already do that?"

Martin said: "Yes. But he had to spit out the information first and then the paramedics had to relate it to the hospital."

Elizabeth asked: "Could he have been saved if it hadn't taken so long to get him to the hospital?"

Martin said: "Three minutes is not a long time. We are human after all. How fast do you think humans can think and speak?"

Elizabeth said: "No more questions your honor."

40

DAY 3 OF the trial started with the usual meeting in the judge's chambers for an update on the progress of the trial. Gene agreed to finish his questioning sometime today. The judge couldn't let go by a stern warning about interrupting and proper behavior in court. Gene promised to behave himself.

The judge entered the courtroom and everybody was ready to begin. He said good morning to everybody. They all responded with smiles and a good morning back. Even the court officers had to smile at the judge whenever he did. They knew he was a man of mush behind the robe. Most of them had coffee with him after court or before hand. He said: "Gene, call your next witness please."

Gene said: "I call Jeff Smith to the stand. As Jeff approached the stand he was sworn in by the bailiff. He said: "Do you solemnly swear to tell the truth the whole truth and nothing but the truth so help you God?"

Jeff said: "I do. He took his seat.

Gene said: Please tell the court who you are and how you are connected to this case?"

Jeff said: "I am a neighbor of Baxter and I am here to testify about the children and their prescence on the block."

Gene said: "Tell us about the children and when you first noticed them."

Jeff said: "I have lived in my house for 30 years. I knew the former owners of the house. We had a party for them when they moved."

Gene asked: "Where did they move to?"

Jeff said: "They moved to Los Angeles for some reason. They saw it on TV and thought it would be nice to live there. There was an episode of cops and they said it looked like a safe place to live. I personally disagrees with them, but they went anyway. They moved to Venice California to the beach area. I would never move to California because of the first OJ trial when they were cut off from society for 9 months like that. Then another judge went to the post office to call people in for jury duty. That is a travesty and I won't be tied up in it. If they treat people like that on jury duty they can all die in the next earthquake for all I care." At that point the jury all stood up and applauded his last statement. They were getting ansy to finish and start the testimony. It took 5 minutes to bring calm to the courtroom again. Even the judge stood up and applauded his outburst. They all felt better after they did that. The court officers were laughing and couldn't contain their glee. Finally order was restored. The judge said: "Okay people. We have all had our fun for the day. Let us begin again and try to stay on track.

Jeff said: "My apologies your honor. I just get so fired up about this whole thing that I forget to shut up."

At that point everybody looked at the back door of the courtroom when it opened. It was Lester's twin brother. The judge yelled "Oh Nice!! Now what have we here?" The man took a seat in the back of the court room. The judge said: "You in the back who just walked in. Please stand up." He stood as he was told. He had to. The bailiff was standing right next to him and he gave him such a look that would make the milk go sour. There was no saying no to him. The judge said: "Approach the bench." He said: "The bench sir?" The bailiff escorted him to the edge of the tables at the front. The judge said: "That is far enough sir. Who in blazes are you and why are you here?"

He said: "I am Lester's twin brother. My name is Max McFarland. I am here to support my brother in his trial."

The judge said: "Jeff, do you recognize this man from the house next door?"

Jeff said: "Yes sir. I have seen him around the house."

The judge asked: "Where have you been?"

Max said: "I have been in the military. I am home now because I have finished my tour of duty."

The judge asked: "Did you know about your brother's shenanigans?"

Max said: "No sir. I didn't know until I showed up at the house this morning. Another neighbor told me where I can find Lester."

The judge asked: "Were you aware of your mother's death?"

Max said: "No sir. I just found out. I was overseas in Germany when everything happened."

The judge asked: "Were you physically abused like your brothers?"

Max said: "If I was I have blocked it out. I blocked out my childhood after I left Nevada for the army."

The judge asked: "Do you remember your father beating the crap out of you?"

Max said: "No sir. I don't remember anything happening to me."

The judge asked: "Is there a 3rd one of you running around this earth to surprise me and complicate these proceedings?"

Max said: "No sir. I am it. There was just me and my twin brother. The adopted brother stayed with my mother. Lester left town to go on a year long holiday. He didn't know they would hire him for a job."

The judge asked: "Have you kept in touch with your family while overseas?"

Max said: "I called a few times, but never visited. I was surprised when I got back to the house and there was no phone."

The judge asked: "I must ask you a second time for the record. Did you know your brother was stealing children off the street?"

Max said: "No sir. I knew my mother needed help, but how she got it was not within my knowledge. Baxter told me he had help with mom, but not where he got it or who it was. I just let it drop at that point. I was very relieved about the whole thing."

The judge asked: "Did you have a hand in stealing the children?"

Max said: "No sir. I was off in Germany when all this was going on."

The judge said: "Very well. My condolences on the loss of your mother. You may be seated."

Max said: "Thank you sir."

The jduge asked: "Elizabeth, do you have any questions for this witness?"

Elizabeth said: "Yes your honor. Now Jeff, what kind of neighbor was Baxter and Lester and his mom?"

Jeff said: "They always kept to themselves. I tried to be friendly and neighborly but they never took the bait. He always spoke in that flat tone of his. That expressionless look was creepy to me."

Elizabeth asked: "What about the mother?"

Jeff said: "I saw her sitting on the porch a few times with her cane. She never had much to say. She wouldn't smile either."

Elizabeth said: "What did you do?"

Jeff said: "What could I do? Some people are just sour all the time. I just let it go and told Baxter if he ever needed anything he can always call on one of the neighbors."

Elizabeth asked: "Did Baxter thank you for that?"

Jeff said: "Yes. He thanked me and then I was dismissed from the porch. I just figured that was his personality. He looked like he might have had a brain injury that made him like that."

Elizabeth asked: "What made you think that?"

Jeff said: "It was a well known fact that after a brain injury people tend to lose their personality. Everything changes."

Gene said: "OBJECTION YOUR HONOR Move to strike. This witness is not an expert nor is he a doctor. He has no right to make assumptions like that."

The judge said: "Sustained. The jury will strike that last answer."

Gene said: "Thank you your honor."

The judge said: "Jeff, keep the testimony to that which you can prove and not what you think you know."

Jeff said: "Yes your honor. Sorry about that."

Elizabeth asked: "Jeff, did you talk to someone in town about your new neighbors?"

Jeff said: "Yes. I talked to the sherriff in town. He went over to talk to them. He said he got the same reaction and I did. He too was dismissed from the property. We just prayed for him that whatever was bothering him he would get straightened out."

Elizabeth said: "Thank you Jeff. No more questions your honor."

The judge said: "Gene call your next witness."

Gene said: "I recall the sherriff of Ely, Nevada to the stand. As he approached the judge reminded him that he is still under oath. He is still obligated to tell the truth."

The sherriff took his seat. Gene said: "Sherriff what was Baxter's reaction when he found you on his porch?

The sherriff said: "He just asked what I was doing on his porch. He dismissed me almost right away. I asked if his mother had a stroke. He said yes why would I ask that? I told him to take it easy. If she ever needed to go to the hospital I would need to know what to tell the paramedics. He asked me where was the nearest hospital. I told him the nearest was Ely Community Hospital. They have all the facilities there. Even open heart surgery. The clinic was not overly crowded. He thanked me and sent me on my way."

Gene asked: "Has his mother ever been seen in the hospital?"

The sherriff said: "Not to my knowledge. If she ever got medical attention it wasn't in Ely."

Gene asked: "What about the other members of the family?"

The sherriff said: Nobody has been sent to the hospital with EMS from that family. I would have gotten a report in the sherriff's office if they had."

Gene asked: "Do you trust your staff completely enough that they would never not fill out paperwork?

The sherriff said: "Yes. We are a very cooperative little town."

Gene asked: "What would have been the repercussions for not doing the report?"

The sherriff said: "We would have withheld their pay for a week if they didn't do the paperwork. Our EMS crew is made up mostly of 20 year olds just back from college. Some residents do come back to stay."

Gene asked: "Is there a college in your town?"

The sherriff said: "No sir. There is no college in our town. They have to go south to either Las Vegas or north to Reno. They have multiple colleges in those towns."

Gene asked: "Is there any plans to build a college to keep the residents from leaving?"

The sherriff said: "Right now we don't have the money to build a college. We would rather leave it like a small town free of pollution than get all these new people in. You never know what is coming in."

Gene asked: "What happened to the house that they lived in?"

The sherriff said: "The house was sold and brought with cash in one lump sum."

Gene asked: "Were you suspicious of somebody buying a house with cash like that?"

The sherriff said: "Yes. But this is a nice young working class couple who happened to have won the publishers clearing house sweepstakes. They showed me the stubs that they are getting $10,000 dollars a week for the next year. That is why they never quit their jobs. It will only last for one year. After that money runs out they are back living paycheck to paycheck."

Gene asked: "Was there a welcoming party for them when they moved in?"

The sherriff said: "Yes. We had a welcoming party with burgers and hot dogs. Nobody talked about how much they spent for the house because we are not that kind of town. We believe in privacy. I certainly have never blabbed how much the house was sold for."

Gene asked: "Are you a real estate agent?"

The sherriff said: "No sir. But my brother is. He was out sick one day and asked me to fill in for him. I showed them the house and they brought it on the spot. I told them right away that I was not the real estate agent. We got to know each other very well that day. I called my brother on the phone and asked what should I do. He gave me instructions and the papers were signed the next day. I do know that the lady of the house has diabetes and now all the diner knows it too. They go there a lot.

Gene asked: "Is there a gym in town for the young people to hang out/"

The sherriff said: "No. People in my town walk wherever they need to be. They also drive. We had a town meeting about putting in a gym once. The town rejected it because they figured you are fat because you eat too much. We have a lot of fruit stands and they do a better business than the cakes sales. The supermarket can't keep the tomatoes in stock in the summer."

Gene said: "Thank you sherriff. No more questions your honor."

The judge said: "Elizabeth, do you have any questions for this witness/"

Elizabeth said: "Yes your honor. Now sherriff, do you have anything in town for the young people coming up?

The sherriff said: "Yes. We have a basketball team that meets at the high school every Friday night. They also have a practice every night. If you show up you play."

Elizabeth asked: When did you first figure out something was off with Lester?"

The sherriff said: "I never met Lester before. I don't remember running into him. It was you that brought to our attention the issue that there were 2 people who looked exactly alike."

Elizabeth asked: "Have you ever met Max before?"

The sherriff said: "No. If he ever did drop by it was after dark. The only one I knew of was Baxter."

Elizabeth asked: "Did Baxter put up a fight when you arrested him?"

The sherriff said: "Yes. He wouldn't cooperate for beans. He wouldn't do anything he was told. We were more than happy to turn him over to someone else. When I met Shapiro I wished him good luck with Baxter. After that he wondered what I meant. The jail got a lot quieter after he left."

Elizabeth said: "Thank you sherriff. No more questions your honor."

The judge said: "You may step down sherriff."

41

SINCE IT IS lunch time we will adjourn for one hour for lunch. Everybody return to here by 1:00 for closing arguments. After lunch everybody returned right on time. The judge said: Gene, you may begin when ready.

Gene said: "Thank you your honor. Ladies and gentlemen of the jury. I am what is known as the defense attorney. My client has been accused of a heinous crime and it is up to me to say that is not true. I started out being the attorney for Baxter his brother. Nobody recognized or realized the scar on the forehead until I met Lester up close. At that point everybody suddenly remembered the scar on the head. If I hadn't mentioned it first it would not have appeared as part of the testimony. I brought this to the attention of Detective Shapiro and he told me to run with it. It was Detective Shapiro that charged my client with kidnapping. He has already admitted to stealing the children, but the charges were never changed to anything else. As usual they flubbed the whole concept of arresting someone. Nobody ever read him his Miranda rights. I tried to do my job by getting Baxter out of jail, but the security guards failed to do their job of protecting him by allowing him to get stabbed. Since the children are now back home with their parents let's leave this to rest. There was no kidnapping because the parents didn't watch their kids properly. One mother hid from view, one wasn't paying attention, and one just let the kid run freely to the bus stop. If anything my client saved the children from disaster. You must find him not guilty on grounds of a technicality. No Miranda warnings, no arrest. They arrested the wrong man the first time around, now they wanted a second try at his brother. They failed again to do their job. Will they ever get it right? Let us say we did everything right the first time. Then we wouldn't be here today. Who is this man to coem out of the blue and say he did something? At that poin the didn't even know his brother was dead. Why did the jail system fail to notify the next of kin? His next of kin was listed as his brother. What was the jail people doing sitting on this duty? Again it was a failure to do their jobs and my client is being held responsible for it. What happened to his brother's body? Nobody has been told. What happened to his mother's body, he hasn't been told?

At this point the judge was turning practically purple with fury. He was wondering if he actually listened to the same trial he was at. The jury noticed this. Elizabeth was looking rather angry herself. The jury noticed that also.

Gene continued, I stand by my statements that Lester

did nothing wrong. Let's talk about the town of Ely first. How come there are no colleges in town? What does he expect people to do with themselves? Of course they will get bored and want to go somewhere else. No wonder there is crime in Ely. Nobody wants to sit home with the 4 walls closing in on them. There is practically no opportunity to advance yourself in that town. My client should be found not guilty of all charges. Thank you all."

The judge said: "Elizabeth, you may begin when ready. Elizabeth said: "Thank you your honor. Ladies and gentlemen of the jury. It has come to the attention of the legal system that Detective Shapiro made a mistake in arresting the wrong man. This may be true. He has never denied it. He made the arrest based on the information he had at the time. It was a psychic who brought the information to the attention of the law enforcement team. If anything she was the one to blame for this mistake. Now a man is dead. You need to find Lester guilty of kidnapping. After all, he already admitted to taking the children. He was never charged with anything else. The sentence you hand down should be consistent with the crime. You should not go to the extreme of saying he should be death be firing squad. You should sentence him to jail for at least 25 years. He is a danger to others. Even though he didn't have a weapon the world is not safe with him in it. One thing we failed to do the first time around is to ask about the scar on his forehead. There was no scar, so there was no need to ask the question. If anything Lester would have gone to his death to allegedly protect the children. From what exactly has never been known. Thank you your honor."

42

A T THIS POINT the judge decided to dismiss the jury for the evening and return to the courtroom the following morning. He gave them strict instructions to not talk about the case, but to think about the evidence that was presented to them and the testimony they heard. They heard a lot of testimony. It was okay if anybody took notes. Nobody thought of that.

At 9:00 the next morning they all returned to the courtroom. The judge said good morning to the jury and told them not to get too comfortable. He reiterated his instructions and they all said they understood perfectly clearly. They assured him nobody talked about the case to anyone. They were ussured into the jury deliberation room, which had a square table with 12 chairs all around. The chairs were wooden chairs and very hard to sit on.

They were also straight backed chairs. The bailiff assigned to supervise explained that this was a tactical maneuver so that the jury wouldn't spend too many days negotiating. They were hoping to get a quick answer to save their own bottoms. At least they had windows to look out on. They were allowed to get up and stretch and walk around the room as much as they wanted to as long as they were back at the table to do the vote. They had to have a unanimous vote in order to convict.

The bailiff said: "We need to elect one juror to be the foreman. That means the one juror hands the piece of paper to the judge and he reads aloud the verdict. Guilty or not guilty. The jury had one brave soul who volunteered for that job. He had experience in it and didn't have a problem doing it. They all agreed to let juror number 5 to do it. Now that that was out of the way they wanted to order breakfast out. They all had scrambled eggs and sausages to eat. Meantime while waiting for the food they started to talk about why they were there. Most of them were totally confused by Gene's closing statements. The bailiff said he was also totally confused. He could not help them along the way. They talked about the speech from Jeff about being sequestered for that long and they all agreed to come to an agreement that day within a few hours. The bailiff was still laughing about the speech. The food arrived and they ate and joked about other things. Then it was down to business. They got serious and started negotiating. Juror number 1 said she thought he was guilty because he admitted it. Juror number 9 asked if that was plausible. She said: " Why would he admit to stealing the kids if he didn't?" Juror number 6 said

Wendy Elmer

he also thought he was guilty. At 12:00 noon they brought it to a vote. It was unanimous that he was guilty. They sent a note to the judge explaining this.

43

WHILE THE JURY was in negotiations Elizabeth and the judge adjourned to his chambers for another blow up. The defense attorney's closing arguments was so confusing he couldn't see straight. He said: "Wasn't it Gene's idea that we bring this up all over again? I thought once Baxter was in jail that would be the end of it. I don't thing he has a legitimate licence to practice law. If he does I suggest having it revoked. He can't even put a sentence together without mucking up the grammar."

Elizabeth said: "I think he does this because if the jury is confused they will just want to find him not guilty and get away from him as soon as possible."

The judge said: "I agree. I wonder if he is really this stupid or if this is an act for the defense table."

Elizabeth said: "I have had coffee with him and I can say this is no act. I think he really is this stupid. Whenever you talk to him he goes off on a tangent and never stays on the subject.

At this point there was a knock on the door from the bailiff that was guarding the jury. He had a note that stated that the jury had a verdict and they were ready to hand it in. He told the bailiff to go next door to where Lester, Gene, and Lester's brother were waiting for word from the jury. They adjourned to the courtroom at 1:00 for the reading of the verdict. The jury filed in. The jduge said: "Has the jury reached a verdict?"

The foreman said: "We have your honor."

The judge said: "Please pass the paper on to me." He held his hand out the judge read it. The judge couldn't help but smile to helself and the jury. This was not allowed, but he couldn't help himself. He said: "Would the defendant please rise?"

Juror number 6 said: "We find the defendant guilty of kidnapping."

The judge asked: "Was this a unanimous vote?"

Juror number 6 said: "Yes sir it is unanimous."

The judge asked: "What about punishment?"

Juror number 6 said we agree to 25 years to life in prison. He is indeed a danger to society."

The judge said: "Ladies and gentlemen of the jury. You are excused. Thank you for your service. You may return to the jury assembly room for your dismissal papers. Good day all."

He turned to Lester and instructed him to go with the court officers and he will be picked up and brought to jail. His lawyer said not to worry about a thing. He will get him out of it soon enough.

44

LESTER'S ARRIVAL AT the jail was a very scary thing for him. He had a shower and had to empty his pockets. His personal belongings were taken and catalogued away for him. He had to shower in front of everybody. He had his first strip search. That was very humiliating. He never thought anybody would look at him like that. He felt that he didn't belong here. He immediately considered suicide because he felt out of place here. He felt that he was there unjustifiably. He was given a sheet set, 3 pairs of boxers, 3 undershirts, and was told he would shower only 3 times a week. He was given his own toothbrush and toothpaste, shampoo, and deodarent. It was not a spray on like he was used to. He met his cell mate about 6 hours after arrival. Lester was given the job of mopping floors like all first time comers. He was paid $1.00 an hour. At least he seemed to get along with his cell mate. His dinner was promptly at 6:00. He was given 15 mintues to eat because of the overcrowding in the jails. He got lucky that his cell mate wasn't trying to kill him or hurt him. He seemed rather civilized. He was just there for mistakes he made that he regretted. He was trying to stay out of trouble and put in his time to get out. Nobody seemed to bother him because he was only there for minor offenses. He wrote bad checks. He couldn't understand how sitting in jail could possibly pay his fines. His dinner consisted of mashed potatoes and canned peas. Since Lester was a health nut he was concerned about the high sodium content of the peas. The guards said there are no snacks to be had in jail at night. He saw the commissary, but he didn't qualify yet to use it. They sold Doritos and potatoe chips and candy, but he had no money in his funds yet. He only got paid $1.00 an hour. He was put on a suicide watch because by the second day he was already making comments about committing suicide. He was put in isolation for his own protection. He was stripped down to his shorts and undershirt and socks. He was assured this is only temporary until he gets straightened out. Lester had to talk to a psychiatrist and his tattoos were removed. This was good because he didn't like the tattoos anyway. He was brought to the infirmary and put to sleep. When he woke up his tattoos were gone. Everybody had a cell search every day to look for tattoo making machines. Lester managed to stay out of trouble by not having any contraband in his cell. He remained in isolation for one year because he was a scared little rabbit. His psychiatric exams revealed period of serious depression and he was put on medication for it. He refused the medication and just kept going downhill.

Finally he was brought in to the infirmary and he was given his antidepressants by way of intravenous drip. He lost a lot of weight because of the side effects. He looked like he was on a hunger strike. He was not helping his medication to take effect. He told his psychiatrist that he was depressed because he was in jail. Swallowing a pill will not change the fact that he was in jail. How was he supposed to feel? The guards explained that he made the choice to kidnap children. He had to pay the consequences. He had to accept his fate. For breakfast he was given toast, scrambled eggs, and 2 tiny sausage links. He said the eggs tasted funny. That was because they were powdered eggs, not real eggs. He had to acquire a taste for them. For lunch he was given a bologna sandwich with nothing on it. Plain and dry. He got lucky to have some orange juice with it. He also had a cup of coffee. Only one, but he was used to four a day. He had to get used to the guards staring at him in the shower. They had to not make it obvious that they were staring at his manliness. He had no opportunity to stuff drugs up his bottom because the guards would never take their eyes off of him. When he went to the psychiatrist he went tied up in chains around his ankles, wrist, groin, and upper thighs. He also had a spit guard on his face. He couldn't breath under there. His breath kept fogging up the plastic and he couldn't see where he was going. He kept tripping up the stairs over the chains around his ankles. The guards had to keep picking him up off the stairs. Then he tripped over the rubber soles of his slip on shoes. Sometimes he was switched to paper slippers, which was worse because the stairs had some design on the grating. He kept thinking his feet were bleeding because it hurt to climb the stairs. One year after his arrival he finally lost his mind and karate kicked the guards. He couldn't take it anymore. The psychiatrist, the walk up the staris with the chains, the lack of food, nutritious food at that. He couldn't take the shower only 3 times a week. He had to have clean shorts on everyday. The guards couldn't believe they were overpowered by this prisoner. He had superman strength out of nowhere. He was restrained by 4 guards and had to be put in a straight jacket to calm him down. He was carried to the infirmary and thrown into a chair. Then he was tied down again. The doctor couldn't believe the trash that was coming out of his mouth. He never heard such words before and so many without a period at the end of the sentence. The guard that he karate kicked was put in the hospital for head injuries. He was returned to work 3 months later. He was still dizzy a lot, but he promised he could manage his job. He was never left alone again with a prisoner. Lester was transferred to a special psychiatric hospital for prisoners. He was diagnosed with split personality disorder confounded by the clinical depression. He tried to be cooperative, but the evil side of him was very nasty and mean. Which side of him came out depended on what the situation was.

He served out the rest of his life sentence in the psychiatric hospital. He went to the "playroom" and therapy room for 3 hours a day. In the playroom he met other prisoners who were in a lot worse shape than he was. They were playing with invisible friends and ping pong with themselves. He saw one man who talked endlessly and refused to shut up.

Lester had enough brain cells left to express that he wanted to eat healthy foods. He wanted whole foods. The admissions director assured him he would eat broccoli and tomatoes and banannas. Those were proper whole foods. Lester knew he was right. He did better in the psychiatric hospital because he had some control over his life. They gave him whole foods and he agreed to take his medication as given. He never relented on that promise. He was given not a hospital robe, but a striped suit of a prisoner.

During therapy Lester was forced to face his demons from the past. He had to explore why his parents beat him senseless. He found that extremely difficult. He was completely unwilling to explore that avenue of his life. His brother Max was called in to help with that process. He came in and was told to sit down and make himself comfortable. They did role playing. It involved one played the parent and one played the child. Hitting and physical contact was not allowed. Lester was put under hypnosis to draw out the demons. At first he was brought back in time to the day he stole the children. Then he slowly stepped back in time to the days when he was beaten. The therapist said that he didn't want to bring him back too soon. It would shock his psyche. Lester remembered the rough play with his brother. He had trouble understanding why Max played so roughly. The slightest provocation and Max took it overboard. Baxter was no help either. He was the same way. Lester grew up wondering why his big brothers picked on him all his life. He wondered what he ever did to them. Max and Lester spent one month of therapy answering that question. Max admitted to seeing Baxter do drugs right in the house. He started smoking at the age of 10 and breathing in that second hand smoke made his brain stop developing. Max and Baxter needed an outlet to let go of the anger they felt at their mother and father. Unfortunately Lester was that outlet.

When Max was under hypnosis it was his turn. He overheard his parents calling him and Lester and Baxter stupid. It was the anger he felt that they thought of them like that. When Lester slapped his mother in her face Max thought that was the best thing he ever did. The beatings stopped and he felt a little bit of jealousy that he didn't have the nerve to actually try that. Their parents never said they loved them. They always felt in the way. Back in those days running away from home was unheard of. They knew once they got caught they would be beaten again. Max remembered one incident where Baxter played the choking game with Lester. Apparently Lester lost brain cells permanently from a lack of oxygen.

Max never did get married. He was afraid if he did and had kids what he would do to them. He explained that the cycle of violence had to stop somewhere. If he got mad he didn't want to beat his own kids black and blue.

Three years into Lester's incarceration into the mental hospital there was an escape attempt by another inmate. He was aided by Lester. His room mate dug a whole into the air conditioning unit. He crawled through the walls and came up to a dead rat. His room mate got so freaked out that he started screaming and all the nurses heard him. They couldn't find him, but his screams were loud and clear. They ran into his room and found Lester screaming into the big hole in the wall. The poor man panicked and couldn't move fast enough. He had enough light to see his way around because each room had lights on. He finally found his way back into his room and they were both put to bed in isolation. There was no air conditioning units in there. Just 4 blank walls and no window. The air was pumped in under the door. Also through the food slot in the door. He had no contact with the outside world for a while. The next day they had to go before the head of administration and explain themselves. They were separated for the rest of their time in there. Since Lester was in for 25 years to life there was no point in adding anymore time. The punishment was once more stripped down to the shorts and socks and paper gown. He was not given any privacy. He had to use the toilet in full view of the guards. His room mate got an extra 15 years tacked on to his sentence. He was given his meals through the slot and he ate in his room. At least he wasn't on a timer of 15 minutes to eat. He never caused any trouble for the guards. His room mate was transferred to another prison so he doesn't get into trouble. He was sent to Alaska where they had the facilities to take care of people like that.

Lester made friends with his brother and forgave his parents. It was hard and took at least a year to exorcise the demons of his soul.

45

ABOUT A WEEK after the trial was over Detective Shapiro was in his morning meeting with his partners. They were going over the cases and which ones to work on. The phone jangled in his ear and he let out a scream of astonishment. It was the Police Commissioner of Las Vegas Police Department. He got startled and stood at attention. His 2 partners also got excited and stood up with him at attention. All the people in the room saw this and stood up at attention. Everybody did that in the presence of the Police Commissioner. He had very good news for Shapiro. John was being promoted to the rank of Detective. The ceremony was set to take place in the Police Academy Gymnasium. His assignment was to inform John of this unexpected development. Shapiro was to report to the ceremony location and be punctual. He was the one who was going to pin him. John earned this promotion by finding the 5 missing children on his own. He knew enough to follow his instinct and do what sometimes sounds outrageous. It got the job done.

Shapiro said: "Yes sir. Thank you sir. Whatever you need sir." After he hung up the phone he made the announcement that John was to be promoted to Detectives. He was currently on mounted police patrol. He would continue that until the day of the ceremony. Everybody in the room applauded with excitement. Shapiro took off the rest of the day and showed up at horse stables and waited for John to return from his workday. He entered the room and Shapiro saw the horse first. The horse remembered Shapiro and started to lick him. Shapiro said: "Good afternoon John. I need to have a word with you right away."

John said: "Let me put the horse away and you can help me undress him.

Shapiro learned a lot that day about taking care of horses. He learned that the saddle had a buckle on his belly and the bridle comes off the nose. The reigns also come off at night. He learned how to wash down the horse and how to measure out the food and water. He learned how to hang the water in the stall without it spilling all over the place. He also learned how to clean the stall and where the poop goes exactly. Apparently he uses a big shovel and throws it into the garbage can. The horse liked John and he was very accepting of Shapiro's presence.

Shapiro said: "Now John for the real reason I came here. I got a phone call from the police commissioner and he said he wants to promote you to Detective. You have been assigned to my squad. You will work with me and from now on I am your boss. I am like the commanding officer. Do you have any questions?"

John said: "I have several questions. What does a detective do exactly?"

Shapiro said: "Exactly what you did for the missing children's case. You followed your instincts and didn't let the locker room teasing stray you away from what you thought was right. You didn't let me get you away from what you thought was right."

John asked: "When is this ceremony that you speak of?"

Shapiro said: "It is on May 31st, 2010 at the police academy gymnasium."

John asked: "Do I have to go ahead of time for any reason?"

Shapiro said: "You have to report to the Police Academy on the 20th for reviews and preparation of the ceremony. There will be inspections to make sure you are physically fit. You also have to have a medical exam to make sure you are physically fit for duty."

John asked: "Can I invite people?"

Shapiro said: "You can invite as many people as you want. You have never talked about family, but you can invite the manager of the Motel 6 and if you have any other close friends or neighbors you can invite them too."

John said: "Thank you very much for everything you have done for me."

46

O N MAY 20TH John arrived at the Police Academy for one week of training and reviews. He had to hang his clothes in the closet and make everything military neat. He filled his foot locker with his underpants, undershirts, and socks. He had no time to read a book, so he didn't even bring one. That was tougher than the review training. Not reading for a week. His shoes and sneakers had to be spit shine polished so that he could see his face in them. He rose at 5:00 a.m. and did exercises. His sit ups and pushups were the judgement as to whether or not he was physically fit. Then he ran around the gym a few times. He ran around the campus and the drill seargents timed him. He came out on top in every exam. The had written exams in the afternoon. Lunch was at 12:00 noon to 12:45. He couldn't wait to get to bed. Bedtime was 9:00 at night. The seargents in charge were very conscious of how much sleep the recruits got. One person was on duty making sure they didn't sneak out. There was one person on each end of the hall. Then there was one person posted on the front desk. They were free to shower and brush their teeth and use the toilet during lights out. But that was all they were allowed to do. No socializing at all. They were sleeping too deeply to have time to do any of that.

Two days before the ceremony they started rehearsing for the dos and don'ts of what to do. Nobody has ever had any experience in this. They had to run through the whole ceremony at least 5 times and practice marching in. During the practice runs there was another inspection. They seemed to do it while the men were in training so they couldn't fix what was wrong. It was their job to be prepared. That was the motto of the Detectives Squad. They practiced walking in properly and they had to make sure their formal uniforms were in perfect condition. No wrinkles or anything fuzz or anything of the sort.

47

FINALLY THE BIG day arrived and the gymnasium was full to the brim. Even the balcony was full to the brim. Luckily there were no tickets involved to be had. They learned that next year they will have to do that. It was really getting out of hand. They were still subjected to following the fire department laws. Overcrowding was not tolerated. They marched in with John leading the group. He again came out on top of the class. He came in with his formal cap, white gloves, spit shine shoes. The pace of the ceremony depended on him. He was also considered the valedictorian of the class. It was amazing that they only had one week of schooling and they were detectives. Shapiro corrected him and said his one week was of ceremony training. The rest was reviews of things he already knew.

The ceremony started with the bagpipes coming in and blowing the roof off the building. The audience exploded into applause to be heard over the bagpipes. The manager of the Motel 6 was there to see John to this promotion. He was very proud of his accomplishments. Surprisingly Mary Kelly also showed up to share in this day in his life. He felt ashamed of not calling her recently.

The police commissioner came in and started the ceremony. He started with the Pledge of Allegiance and then they all were seated. The audience was invited to stand and recite with them. Then the Police Commissioner started the announcements. He called John up to the stage for a valedictorian speech. John got up and went up on stage.

He said: "I started out in jail and the guards and psychiatrist really helped me to straighten my life out. After I got out they wished me God speed and drove me to Las Vegas to the Motel 6 where I still work on the weekends. Then I got my first own apartment and my own shopping in a supermarket for my groceries. It was then that I met Detective Shapiro in the bread aisle. He suggested that I become a cop. I didn't think about that because I was already in jail. I had a criminal record, but only for minor offenses. For the first time in my life I had a direction and reason to get up in the morning. I also see Mary Kelly in the audience. I consider these people member of my family because I am single and never had my own. If it wasn't for them I would never have been where I am now. I want to sincerely thank them for helping me get to this point in my life. I would like them to stand up and show yourselves. I have never been good in expressing myself. I solved the case of the missing 5 children because I was called in to Detective Shapiro's office for a consultation. The most important thing to remember is that there should always be time for reading. I haven't read a book in a week. That is what I miss most from my training. I always came up on top, but maybe because I read a book an hour a day. You are in charge of your children's actions. I never knew I was so competent about anything until I found people who believed in me. If it wasn't for me answering the call of a psychich these children would never have been found. Shapiro told me not to waste my time, but I didn't listen. He thought I was crazy. I didn't listen. I pray to God that I can make a judgement on the next case. My favorite experience was being a mounted cop. I learned about dressing a horse and proper care of a horse. If you are told you are nuts, just say Thank you sir. To me I just filed that away and moved on. My first experience with mounting a horse was a disaster. I ended up facing the tail end of the horse. It took my seargeant 20 minutes to stop laughing at that one. Please take time to laugh at yourself. You are your own biggest entertainment. I was so embarrassed and felt so stupid that I wanted to crawl under the horse. He would have seen me anyway. Again this was a situation where people actually believed in me and enjoyed my company. I still see one of the children in the supermarket. I learned all about the Code Adam and searching a building from top to bottom. I have met a nun who was very beautiful in spirit. I have never seen her head. She is covered with a cap and an old fashioned nun's dress. I have learned that you can learn a lot from children in the 1st grade. They are of beautiful minds and very curious. Don't eliminate people because of what they look like or appear to be. Please do not tell your grandchildren that little children should be seen and not heard. I thank you for listening to me and hope you take into consideration what I have said. To recap it is this. Read, Listen to other people, and Be Open to learning from other people.

The audience applauded for 5 minutes and then sat down and the ceremony continued. The police commissioner stood up and asked Detective Shapiro to come up and pin John. He did so and there was a handshake and a picture taken of John and the Police Commissioner. There was another one taken that included Detective Shapiro with the Police Commissioner. It took 45 minutes to pin everybody because everybody needed a picture with the Police Commissioner. They had to hand the pin to the family member and the family member had to pin it on the recipient. At the end everybody stood up and the new detectives threw their caps in the air and celebrated. There was coffee and tea and cakes afterwards in the other gymnasium. There was juice for the children.

John was given a week off for vacation and the returned to Detective Shapiro's office for his first assignment. The dress code was to dress in a button down shirt and at least a tie. He was still celebrating the promotion a week later. He had a lot of parties. The manager, the building manager and they all took him out for a steak dinner. He learned that Shapiro jumps every time the phone rings. He spills his coffee on his tie all the time. John was told to be careful in filling his coffee cup up. Don't fill it up to the brim. He would look very sloppy going out to the crime scenes with stains on his clothes. He was given the lecture that between cases they didn't do much. Every Monday morning they had a meeting to discuss their progress. He said not to get too spoiled because he solved one case. Don't be afraid to ask for help. He has to not be afraid to fly because sometimes their job takes them outside of the Las Vegas area. The phone rang and there was their next assignment already. It was a problem with the New York New York Hotel. The roller coaster exploded. They were off again. There was no time limit to solving cases, but there is a higher up who tracks how many are really solved. They were off again.

About the Author

This second book has the same characters as the first book. It takes place in Las Vegas, Nevada. Las Vegas was one of my favorite places to visit. The book introduces a horse kneeling at the altar rail of a church. I thought children would like this image. It brings humor to your reading time. I have lived in New York City all my life. I went to Catholic Schools all my life. Reading is always the most important thing you can do with your children. Then I tried writing and saw success, so I continued writing. I am still writing poems whenever they pop into my head. There will be a third book next year. I am attempting to write it now.